RUNAWAY MURDER

MURDER ON THE RAILS ~ BOOK ONE

DIANA ORGAIN

D1523407

Lemonade
Press

OTHER TITLES BY DIANA ORGAIN

Third Time's a Crime If only love were as simple as murder...

ROUNDUP CREW MYSTERY SERIES

Yappy Hour Things take a *ruff* turn at the Wine & Bark when Maggie Patterson takes charge

Trigger Yappy Salmonella poisoning strikes at the Wine & Bark.

iWITCH MYSTERY SERIES

A Witch Called Wanda Can a witch solve a murder mystery?

I Wanda put a spell on you When Wanda is kidnapped, Maeve might need a little magic.

Brewing up Murder A witch, a murder, a dog...no, wait...a man..no...two men, three witches and a cat?

COOKING UP MURDER MYSTERY SERIES

Murder as Sticky as Jam Mona and Vicki are ready for the grand opening of Jammin' Honey until...their store goes up in smoke...

Murder as Sweet as Honey Will the sweet taste of honey turn bitter with a killer town?

Murder as Savory as Biscuits Can some savory biscuits uncover the truth behind a murder?

RUNAWAY

MURDER

A Murder on the Rails Mystery
(Gold Strike Mystery Series)

by
Diana Orgain

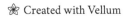

CHAPTER 1

"So how is the new job going anyway?" my best friend Vanessa asked as she swung the cab into the station's car parking lot.

It was already busy, people hurrying through the turnstiles, dragging their luggage or clutching a toddler's hand. I couldn't help but smile. The hustle and bustle of the station always got my heart pumping. It reminded me of my time in Europe as a young adult, when I'd splurged on a Eurail Pass after graduating college. I'd crisscrossed the continent, meeting new people, drinking in experiences, and growing beyond what I'd thought possible. And falling in love for the first time. Yes, I fell in love with travel, Europe, and a sweet, sweet French boy, Laurent.

Trains would forever equal excitement to me.

I got out of the cab without answering Vanessa and looked around, my arm resting on the open door. I found the mix of old and new intoxicating—the state-of-the-art commuter trains next to the luxury vintage carriages that captured people's attentions.

The scent of diesel clung to the air, the quintessential smell of the station complemented by the aroma of summer. Whenever I smelled diesel anywhere else, I was instantly transported back to the station, back to huddles of eager people waiting to discover what their day had in store for them. Back to the thrill I felt every time I stepped onto the train.

The sun was high in the sky, beating down on us mercilessly, and it brought with it that peculiar feeling of possibility and hope that summer always brought. I raised my face, embracing the warm rays with my smile, and I let the now-familiar sounds wash over me: the chatter and excitement of the passengers, the whistle of the station master, the gentle thrumming of the trains as they awaited their guests. And in the background, my own train chugged, steam rising up from the vent as it idled on its track.

I say *my* train, but of course it wasn't mine. It felt like it though, even then, after only two months of working on it. It'd already become a second home to me, and one I'd fallen in love with. It was an old-style steam engine, controlled by a brilliant team of technicians and engineers, all wearing retro uniforms. Every day, we would wind our way through forty miles of majestic redwood forests, scenic mountain meadows, and over thirty trestle bridges in Northern California, and every day, it took my breath away.

Gold Country.

Me? I was the chef—the first ever female executive chef of the Western Rails train, actually, and I had a passion for every part of my job, from the train itself to the scenery around us and the luxury experiences we offered our customers. I woke up eager to go to work every day and to experience the adventure that lay before us, every trip different than the last.

"Hello? Earth to Jessica?" Vanessa said.

"What?" I turned to face Vanessa, shaking myself out of my reverie, but she was still in the car, calling from the driver's seat. I bent down and peered in. "Sorry, Ness. What did you say?"

Vanessa chuckled. "I asked how your new job's going," she said, looking up at me. "You all right?"

"Yeah, of course," I said. "Hey, I have an idea. Are you very busy today?"

She shrugged. "Not super, for a change," she said. "No bookings until later on tonight when the train returns to the station. What've you got in mind?"

"You want to know how my job is going, right? Why don't you come along for the ride? You could do with the break—I know this influx of tourists has been stressing you out—and if you've got no fares booked, you might as well take a few hours off and enjoy the countryside."

"I'm *not* stressed," she insisted.

I rolled my eyes. Of course, she was stressed. She was the only cabbie in the town of Golden, and it was getting busier by the day. If she wasn't careful, she'd be on course for a nervous breakdown, and that worried me. She'd never admit it though; she was far too pig-headed for that.

"All right, Ness, you're not stressed," I said to placate her. "How about this then. I would like to spend some time with my best friend since I haven't seen her properly for weeks. There's a stool in the kitchen with your name on it, and I might even be able to scratch up an extra burger or two . . ."

I raised my eyebrows at her as she thought through the offer, but it was only a matter of seconds before she smiled sheepishly, shrugged her shoulders, and agreed.

"Okay then," she said with a girlish giggle bubbling from her lips. "You've persuaded me. It'll be nice to do something different. And you can tell me what you think about my heist theories!"

I smiled at her as I waited, but she didn't move. "So . . . you going to get out of the car, then?" I asked.

"Oh, right!"

She threw her head back in a laugh, then clambered out of the car and slammed the door closed. I loved Vanessa like a sister, but she had never been graceful, and it made me smile to see it. It was typical Vanessa. She was stout rather than big, and a good foot shorter than me. Her yellow-blonde hair seemed always to be tied into a messy bun and she rarely wore makeup, but at fifty-two years old, her cheeks were still flushed with a youthful energy and her eyes sparkled with laughter and delight.

I grabbed my bag from the back seat and flung it over my shoulder, happy to have her accompany me for the day. I was not lying when I said I hadn't seen her for weeks, and I was beginning to miss her company. Besides, I wanted to show her just what a magnificent journey I made each and every day.

"So, heist theories?" I asked as I led Vanessa through the throngs of people toward the staff entrance. I tapped in the security code and listened for the click of the door unlocking.

"Morning, Jessica," the guy on reception said as soon as I pushed open the door. "And Jessica's friend." I guessed he'd seen us on the security camera—at least, he always seemed to know who was entering even before they entered. He had to be seventy if he was a day, and I'd never seen him out of that chair. Bob knew everyone and everything that went on in the station, and he never had a bad word to say about anyone.

"Morning, Bob," I replied brightly.

"Big day today," he said, nodding at me with a serious expression.

"Yeah, but we're ready for it," I said. "You know us, Bob. Dream team and all that."

"You get 'em, girl," he said with a grin that reminded me of my father. *Girl* was not a word often used to describe me anymore, not with the fifty-five years I had behind me. From anyone else, it might have felt patronizing, but from Bob, it was endearing.

"Big day?" Vanessa asked as we passed through the building and out onto the platform.

"It's the Annual Summer BBQ Excursion," I said over my shoulder, making it sound as grand as it felt. "The locals love it. I reckon we'll have a fair number of regulars on that train today. Greg says this excursion is always a hoot."

"I'm not going to be in your way, am I?" Vanessa asked, shooting me a worried glance. "If it's such an important day and all. Even I've heard of the summer barbecue."

"Don't be silly," I replied. "Everything's already prepared. Besides, it's only barbecue chicken and corn on the cob. What could go wrong?"

"Well, if you're sure . . ."

"I'm sure," I said firmly. "No getting out of it now, Vanessa Scott. We've got some catching up to do!"

"Excuse me," a young woman said, slipping past us and through the crowds. I stepped out of the way.

"You've heard about the heist, right?" Vanessa asked, pulling me back to the conversation we hadn't quite started earlier on.

"Of course I have," I said, moving out of the way of a well-dressed man pulling an enormous trunk. He looked like something out of the 1920s, like I'd somehow stepped back in time, and I stifled a chuckle. How delightful!

"Hey," I said. "Would you like a hand with that?"

"Sure," he replied. "Thank you."

I leant down and grabbed the handle on the far end of the trunk, swinging my bag around my back. "Where to?" I said once it was in the air.

"Luggage locker," he replied, nodding over to the small room in the far corner. "I had to check out of my hotel early this morning. I sure was glad when I found out I didn't have to lug it around with me all day!"

"Yeah, there are some pretty great resources here at the station." Vanessa ran ahead of us and opened the door. "And I hope you don't mind my saying, but I *love* your trunk."

"Not very convenient, like these modern ones with wheels," he admitted. We put the trunk down and he grinned as we straightened up. "But I never was one for all things modern. Thanks for your help."

"No worries," I said. "Maybe catch you later."

"Morning, Jessica," another man cried as soon as we were back on the platform. He was suited and booted and ready for a long day in the office. He waved a hand in the air. I waved back. I never had learned his name, and I didn't really know how he'd learned mine, but he was on this platform every morning at the same time, and he always said good morning.

"So, what do you think?" Vanessa asked, hot on my heels as I worked my way past people.

"About what?" I asked over my shoulder, and she tutted loudly.

"The heist, of course!"

Ah yes, the heist. It had been on everyone's lips since it happened, only two nights earlier. Golden's small but historic museum had been broken into, and someone had stolen the golden spike the town had been loaned to commemorate the transcontinental railroad's 150th anniversary.

"That spike was 17.6 karats. Er . . . is . . . wherever it's ended up."

I laughed and flicked my long black hair over my shoulder. I had to keep it tied up when I worked, so I liked to wear it down whenever I could.

"Yes, I saw the exhibit too," I said before parroting the words that had gone around the town ever since we received news of the artifact's arrival. "Driven into the First Transcontinental Railroad by Leland Stanford himself in 1869."

"And now someone's stolen it!" Vanessa squeaked.

I stopped and turned to look at her, both amused and endeared by how much she cared. The news had rocked the town to its core, and Vanessa did love a good mystery, but this one seemed to have gotten to her personally.

"Yes, it's an awful business," I replied. "But they'll find who did it and return the spike to its rightful place, I'm certain of it. Golden PD will put the best people on the job."

I rubbed her arm and smiled at her, then turned and continued through the station. I could almost hear her rolling her eyes at me before she started walking again.

"Best people my a—"

"Vanessa," I warned with a chuckle.

"Arm," she insisted, pulling up beside me. "I was going to say arm! And anyway, who cares if they've Sherlock Holmes himself on the case. Doesn't stop *us* theorizing, does it? I do love a good theory."

I snorted at that, unable to stop myself, but I didn't answer. I was sure to hear all her wild and wonderful theories throughout the day.

"Good morning, Jessica," a woman said, a thick bag strap across her chest as she strode across the platform. Mary was a ticket collector, and bright and breezy as always.

Vanessa stopped and looked all around her, her face crumpled in a question.

"What is it?" I asked, turning back to her.

"Everyone knows you," she said.

"Golden's a small town," I replied with a shrug. "And I'm here every day. It's nothing, really."

I said that, but in truth, I loved that everyone knew my name. It gave me that warm feeling, like I belonged. I liked to nod a greeting at the track inspectors gathered around in their hi-vis jackets, looking as though they were discussing something of great importance. I said hello to a conductor as he climbed aboard a train, and again to the signalman at the end of the platform. Along with all the passengers— both known and new—we felt like a true community, almost a town in our own right.

"Well, anyway," Vanessa said. "I've been thinking a lot about it."

"The heist?" I asked as we skipped down the steps to the underground tunnel—a must to get to our own platform. It was quiet down there, as it always was, the walls and ceiling insulating the space from the noise above. It was echoey, too, so when Vanessa spoke again, I jumped and threw a hand to my chest.

"The security must have been terrible," Vanessa said. "I mean, it's understandable in a small town like Golden, but you'd think they would have kicked it up a notch, given the spike was there."

"This way," I said, turning and trotting up a set of steps.

"Even so, I reckon the person who did this was experienced. Must have been, right? He—or she—has done this before. I think . . ."

She stopped talking as we came out onto the platform. It was busy here, too, though less so. There was a relaxed atmosphere, people milling around as though on vacation, smiling and chatting to each other and making friends. And there, gently puffing away, was the train.

"It's . . ."

"Beautiful?" I suggested.

"Impressive, certainly."

She had seen it before, of course, but never up close. I always loved to see people's reactions when they first saw it. It was an old train, but it had been revamped and brought into the modern world. It ran on steam, but inside it had all the features of a brand-new train. And from the outside, it looked as though it had just rolled out of the manufacturers for the first ever time.

The station master blew his whistle—two short puffs—a first reminder to get onboard. The end door opened, and out leaned the general manager, Greg, holding onto the handle. He grinned wildly, then looked at us.

"Come aboard, ladies. Come aboard."

CHAPTER 2

"*M*orning, Greg," I muttered as I made my way up the metal steps, my footsteps clanking as I went.

He didn't move at first, asserting his dominance by making me brush past him, I'm sure. But one quick glare from me had him hopping onto the platform to give us space.

"Good morning, Jessica, and what a lovely morning it is, too."

"What's got into you this morning?" I asked.

He was always either far too happy or far too irritable, never in between, although part of me was convinced he acted the temperamental boss for my benefit.

"Can a man not be happy at work, Jess?" he asked.

I just shook my head and walked past into the waiting area as Vanessa pulled herself up. Greg Kendrick was one of the less pleasant parts of my job. He was the train's chief conductor and general manager—and *my* ex-lover.

Our affair had been brief, and long before I took the job on the train, but there was no escaping the fact that it had happened. I hadn't been in the best of places after my divorce,—and even though my two kids and my stepson had long ago flown the nest, I'd still felt guilty divorcing their father. Greg had been a nice distraction from all that, but boy, had it come back to haunt me when I started working on this train.

Whenever he disagreed with me or refused to entertain my ideas—which was often enough—I wondered whether he was punishing me for ending things when I did. I quickly put that thought out of my mind, though. Greg was a lot of things, but he was always a consummate professional. He loved that train as much as I did, and after two months on the job, I was beginning to get a handle on him and his temperament.

Vanessa widened her eyes as she looked at me, and I shot her a questioning look back. When we were halfway through the first carriage on our way to the kitchen, she spoke over my shoulder.

"He still holds a torch for you," she said.

"Who? Greg?" I tutted. "Don't talk nonsense."

"It's not nonsense," Vanessa insisted. "Did you see the way he looked at you?"

"Anyway, about that heist," I said, knowing full well it would divert the topic.

"Yes, about that . . ."

Her crazy criminal theories were a whole lot better than her romance theories, and she was wrong, anyway. The only person Greg held a torch for was Greg himself, and even if he *did* still have feelings for me, they certainly weren't reciprocated.

"You've seen the Batman movies, right?"

"Er . . . yeah, I think so," I replied, having no idea where this was going.

"You know that grapple hook thingy he uses to swing from buildings?"

"Yeah," I said slowly.

"I reckon our thief had one of those."

I snorted with laughter. "So, he breaks into the museum, snatches the spike, then climbs up onto the roof, throws a grapple hook, and swings to safety, all without anyone noticing? In a tiny town like Golden?"

"Well, think about it," Vanessa urged. "The spike is what? Five, maybe six inches long? Small enough to fit in a pocket. He's already set off the alarms, and the security guards are walking the perimeter, right? There's no way he was getting out through the front or back doors. From the roof is the only way."

"She's not wrong," a voice said, and I stopped, surprised.

It was Carter Osborne, one of the train's regulars. I often wondered what he did with his life, because he didn't seem to work much, other than writing his great literary novel that never seemed to get any further than a page or two. He was a short man with thick glasses and an overbite. He liked to talk too. While he was friendly enough, he liked most of all to share his ideas on how to improve the train—new seat covers, a different event, music piping through the carriages. He even went so far as to advise the engineers on how to do their job—much to their irritation.

"Morning Carter," I replied with a smile. "Nice to see you today."

"Wouldn't miss it for the world," he said. "One of my favorite days of the year, this. And your friend is quite correct; there's no way the thief would have got out through the front of the building."

Vanessa puffed up. "Thank you very much, Mr. . . ."

"Osborne. Carter Osborne," he said, holding a hand out. Vanessa shook it gratefully, throwing me one of her *I told you so* looks.

"Enjoy the day, Carter," I said chuckling and tugging on Vanessa's arm to encourage her further into the train.

"Now, he seems like a very nice guy," Vanessa said.

"Only because he agreed with you," I said with a chuckle.

"Regular?" she asked.

"Yep. A writer. Or he's trying to be, anyway. He signed up for this scheme where he gets to ride the rails for free in return for a bit of social media publicity, but he's got, like, two followers or something."

"He's not as daft as he looks, then," Vanessa said. "Free train rides and no work. What's he writing?"

"Who knows?" I said. "I'm pretty sure his ideas change by the day!"

The interior of the train had been designed with luxury in mind. At the head, there was the motorcar, where all the workings were. It was hot and loud and full of activity for the entire journey. The next carriage housed Greg's office—somewhere I found myself often—and a small infirmary that was, thankfully, rarely used, along with guest facilities. There were two passenger coaches with carpeted floors and leather couches, all facing inward. The windows were draped with blue velvet curtains, held back by golden ropes. After that was my domain: two restaurant cars and the kitchen.

"All right, if not a grapple, then what?" Vanessa asked.

"Good morning," I said brightly to a couple who seemed deeply in love, snuggled together on one of the couches and gazing out of the window. "Maybe he flew, Ness?"

"Don't be so ridiculous," Vanessa replied, shaking her head.

I pulled open the oak-paneled door at the end of the coach, stepping over the join and entering the next.

"Okay, okay," I said, holding my hands in the air. "In all seriousness, then. How he escaped is not all that important, is it? I mean, surely where he is now and *who* he is are the questions we should be asking."

"Fair point," Vanessa conceded.

About halfway through this coach, a woman leapt up from her seat and blocked our path. She was tall and well-dressed, perhaps fifty or so years of age. Her hair, though graying, had been twisted into an elegant knot, with strands hanging down to frame her face. She held herself proudly, hands clasped neatly in front of her, and given the state of her dress, I would say she was a paramour of the finer things in life.

"You must be Jessica Preston," she said. "The chef. Your reputation precedes you."

She thrust her hand in my direction, and I stared at it for a moment before taking it and shaking it slowly.

"Thank you. Yes, that would be me."

She waved her hand in the air dismissively. "My name is Mrs. Beverly Lyonel, and I'm visiting Golden from Napa. I was hoping to ask you a few questions about the town."

"You a journalist or something?" Vanessa asked. "Because if you are, you've got to write about the museum heist."

Mrs. Lyonel offered her a weak smile, an unconvincing one, and that irritated me. She turned to face me again, making a point that she was talking to me and me alone.

"I'm considering moving here to start a new winery. I unfortunately lost my old one, which had been in my family for generations, in the canyon fires earlier this year."

"I'm sorry to hear that, Mrs. Lyonel, but I have to get to the kitchen."

"I only have a few questions," she said, stepping further into the aisle.

Not one to be easily accosted, I took a step closer to her, making it clear I wanted to pass.

"Mrs. Lyonel, the start of any journey is the busiest time. I will come and find you later on during the trip, and I promise I will answer all your questions."

"Oh, but it won't take long," she said, pulling a sheet of paper from her bag.

"Really, Mrs. Lyonel," I said, more firmly this time. "I must get on, but I assure you I will help in any way I can once the barbecue preparations are underway."

I took another step forward, and thankfully, Mrs. Lyonel stepped aside, but not without a confused look on her face.

"Barbecue?" she asked, her voice high-pitched.

"Yes," I replied as I passed her with a smile. "Today's feast . . . The Annual Summer Barbecue Excursion."

I could feel her frowning at my back as I carried on down the aisle, but I forced it out of my mind. Perhaps I had been a little harsh with her; she'd been friendly enough, and she was only looking for help, but I hated when people snubbed my friends

"She was a bit of a busybody, wasn't she?" Vanessa muttered into my ear, and my lips tightened as I suppressed a smirk.

By the time we got to the kitchen, I'd said hello to several more passengers and been caught in two more conversations. As I put my bag down on the counter and pulled my hair into a ponytail, I sighed with the relief of being in the place I loved best—my kitchen.

"Your stool's over there," I said to Vanessa, nodding at the corner as I slipped my chef's whites on over my simple jeans and tee combo I always wore to work.

I tied my apron around my waist and pulled my hat down from the shelf, though I didn't put it on yet. The passengers liked to see me in the traditional garb, so I had one of those big puffy chef hats rather than the simple, modern caps I was used to. I didn't mind; it sort of fed into the fantasy I'd had as a child—I'd always wanted to be a chef.

Before starting on the train, I'd worked in many different restaurants, serving everything from simple fare to fine dining and everything in between. I'd catered for all the town's big events for years too —from Living History Day to the Fourth of July Parade. So when this job came up, it seemed only natural that I applied for it—and even Greg had to admit I was the best qualified out of all the candidates.

Vanessa looked around approvingly. "Nice place you've got here. I can see why you like it so much."

I stopped what I was doing and looked around too, unable to keep the smile from my face. I sighed in satisfaction. I loved every part of my job, but my kitchen was my sanctuary. Being on a train, it was a lot smaller than any other kitchen I'd worked in, and at first, I wasn't sure how I'd cope with it. Now, though, I reveled in its compactness— everything was at hand and in easy reach, and it forced me to be a lot more organized.

And most of all, I loved the huge window that made up one wall, countertops running just below it. As we made our way through the countryside, it felt like I was cooking right there in the middle of the forest. If I was having a bad day—which was rare now, admittedly—all I had to do was look out over the valleys and I'd be in heaven again.

"You just wait and see what it's like when we get going. You'll be itching to sell your cab and get a job here," I said with a chuckle.

"Maybe it was the mayor," Vanessa said, ignoring my idea. She plonked herself down on the stool, hooking the small heel of her boots on the ring around the bottom.

"The mayor? Why on earth would he want to steal the golden spike?"

"Maybe he has money trouble," Vanessa said conspiratorially. "*Maybe* he's in debt and has managed to keep it a secret. Think about it —he had access to the spike, he knew the security routines, and no one would suspect him."

"No one would suspect him because there was no way it was him,"

I said as I slid my bag into the locker under the counter. "I mean, come on. Mayor Foster? No way."

"Yeah," she replied, looking down at the floor with her chin all screwed up. "You're right. He's too much of a good guy."

I pulled the door of the chiller open, then peered inside and smiled; everything was there, just as planned. "You may be onto something with the money troubles thing though. Maybe that would get us to our thief."

"*Our* thief?" Vanessa laughed. "Thought you weren't interested. They've got the best people on the job, remember?"

I squirmed. She'd got me. I always tried to keep out of these things, but once I began thinking about them, I couldn't stop. I loved a good puzzle as much as Vanessa did, I just didn't allow myself to indulge so easily.

"Morning," Penny sang as the door swung open and she sauntered in, Amy just behind her.

"Morning, both," I said. "Hope you're ready for a busy day!"

"Always," Amy replied.

They were my dream team, my hand-picked staff members who helped make our little transcontinental restaurant a huge success. At sixteen years old, Penny was a pot washer and an apprentice of sorts, learning the tricks of the trade whenever we had a spare five minutes. She was slim and pretty, with hair so blonde it was almost white and bright blue eyes that shone with life.

At thirty-six, Amy was older and quite a bit more sensible. Her hair was the color of chestnuts and her eyes the same shade. She'd started off as a waitress, but now she was almost like a partner in crime. She helped me shape the menus and select the best suppliers, and she felt our wins and losses as keenly as I did. The three of us worked closely together, as a team not a hierarchy, and that's just how I liked it.

"Morning," Vanessa said brightly from her corner stool, making Amy jump.

"Goodness," she said with a laughing gasp. "You frightened the life out of me."

"I hope not," I said. "We've got far too much to be getting on with to be dealing with any lifeless bodies today! Anyway, this is my friend, Vanessa. She's coming along for the ride today. And I'll warn you now, she'll have you both talking about that museum heist all day."

"I reckon it was a group," Penny said as she shrugged off her jacket and shoved it in her locker. "I mean, no one person could have done it alone, could they?"

"All these tourists don't help matters," Amy said. "I mean, it's great that Golden's on the map and all, but when I was a kid, everyone knew everyone. We even knew visitors by name! How can they even hope to find the culprit when there are so many strangers in town?"

"See," Vanessa said, shaking her head at me. "Everyone wants to solve this case!"

"Can we at least work while we solve it?" I said, looking around at my team. "Amy, you go get the dining rooms ready. Penny, there's a whole box of corn over there that could do with shucking."

"Oh joy," Penny said, rolling her eyes. "I do love shucking corn."

"Hey, it could be worse," I said.

I leant down and pulled a big saucepan from the storage cupboard beneath the counter and put it onto the stove. I'd make a start on the barbecue sauce, then get the chicken prepped. But as I opened the chiller door, ready to pull out the ingredients I needed, the door swung open again.

"What is it, Amy?" I asked, then turned and started. It wasn't Amy; it was one of the porters.

"Hey, Jessica. Sorry, but Greg wants to see you in his office right away."

"But I'm busy," I replied.

He just shrugged. "He said it was important."

I sighed but went anyway, and as I walked through the door, I heard Vanessa mutter, "I told you so."

CHAPTER 3

$\mathcal{I}$ strode through the train's rocking corridor. We'd pulled away from the station and were slowly building up speed—not that we ever went very fast. These trips were about sitting back and enjoying the ride and forgetting the speed at which we lived the rest of our lives. There was too much haste in the world. We needed to learn to relax again.

My ponytail swung behind me as I walked, my head held high even if my teeth were clenched in annoyance. He'd already seen me once today, albeit briefly on the platform. What did he want to see me again for? We'd butted heads on more than one occasion, and I was only grateful that his office was about as far away from the train's kitchen as it could possibly be.

"Excuse me," Said one of the passengers—on her way to the train's restaurant, probably. We often had early birds wanting snacks or light bites to keep them going until we served the main meal later on in the journey.

I smiled politely and stepped into the doorway to let her pass, feeling the coolness of the air air-conditioning on my back. She was a slight woman, compact, almost fragile looking, though the way in which she held herself told me she was anything but. I'd bet she got that all the time—people assuming she was weak simply because she was small. Her skin was lightly tanned and she wore her hair in a short, dark bob. But it was the way in which she marched down the aisle of the train that caught my attention.

There was something odd about it. Something purposeful, like she had somewhere to be. She acted more like a commuter than a day-tripper, and it seemed to me to be such an odd attitude to have on a luxury experience train like this one. I shook my head as I watched her go through the door at the far end. It must just be the way she was; some people found it difficult to relax.

I made my way through the rest of the train. When I finally reached Greg's office, I took a deep, calming breath before knocking on the door.

"Come in," he called.

I twisted the brass knob and stuck my head around the door, part of me not wanting to go all the way into his office and hoping I would not have to. It was a small, dingy room with papers and notebooks everywhere. It was as far from the luxury of the rest of the train as you could get, and I often wondered how Greg ever found anything in all that mess.

"You wanted to see me?" I said.

"Yes, yes. Come in, Jessica. Sit down."

He smiled bombastically at me, already looking smug, and I reminded myself to just get out of there as quickly as possible. As I sat down, I spotted Walter—the company's computer guru—seated in the corner, looking equally pleased with himself. I looked from one to the other curiously.

"What's going on?" I asked, a sense of unease growing in the pit of my stomach.

Greg laughed. Actually laughed! It was a habit of his that I'd hated when we were seeing each other, and I hated it even more now. What sort of person laughs randomly like that? I bit the inside of my cheek, reminding myself I would be out of the office and back in my beloved kitchen before I knew it. I'd whip up a pie—I always liked to bake when I was stressed, much to the delight of our passengers.

"Good news," Greg said. "Good old Walter here has found a way of doubling ticket sales."

"Has he, indeed?" I asked, shooting Walter a look. He shrugged almost apologetically, and I had to remind myself that none of this was his fault.

"Yes," Greg continued. "You must have noticed how busy the train is today?"

I had, he was right, but it was the Summer Excursion. "They're here for the barbecue," I said simply. "Didn't you say these excursions were always popular?"

He laughed again and rubbed at the dark stubble on his chin that always seemed the same length, no matter the time of day. "It seems I was right all along."

I paused, waiting for him to continue, but he obviously wanted me to ask. I rolled my eyes. "About what?" I asked, trying to keep my tone light.

"The tourists are hankering for a fancier feast than the one you currently serve," he said with a grin.

How did I ever find him attractive?

He was handsome enough, I supposed. It was his personality that was the problem. His face was round, but not overly full, and he had long, dark eyelashes over steely gray eyes. I used to feel butterflies in my tummy whenever he looked at me through his lashes, but now I could see it for what it was—an overused gesture that he knew the ladies loved. It was useful for distracting them from his seemingly ever-present smirk.

"Listen, Jessie," he said, putting his elbows onto the desk and pointing at me with his pen.

"Jessica," I corrected.

"All right, Jessica," he conceded. "I love your barbecued chicken, corn on the cob, and baked beans as much as the next man, but I think we've proven—with the sales—that it's just not the fine fare our consumers want."

I hated that word: *consumers*. It turned our friendly, funny, warm passengers into numbers on a spreadsheet. I wasn't sure Greg ever went out to meet them. All they represented to him was dollar signs.

"But the townsfolk adore their Summer BBQ Excursion," I said, even though I'd said it a thousand times before. "You can't take that from them just because a bunch of strangers—"

"It's not the townsfolk who bring in the money, Jessie—"

"Jessica."

"If I may," Walter said, interrupting in that nasally voice of his. "The wine industry in Northern California is booming, thanks to all those canyon fires."

"And is that something to be happy about, Walter? The fires?" I asked, looking aghast at his wide grin. He quickly swapped it for a sympathetic frown, though his eyes were wide with panic. I suspected he was not used to dealing with strong women.

"No, no, no." He shook his head firmly, as though trying to convince me. "That's not what I'm saying at all. What I'm trying to say is—"

"What Walter is saying is that with the area becoming the new wine country, we've got a chance to grab hold of the market. The place is filling up with more and more tourists by the day. We've got to take advantage of that."

"But—"

"But nothing, Jessie. It's been decided." He held his hands in the air helplessly, like he wasn't happy about the result. "We're replacing your simple meal with a gourmet champagne brunch."

"Right." I slapped my thighs then got up from my seat. "Is that all?" I couldn't bring myself to smile again. Not here, and not for Greg. And I wouldn't sit there listening to any more of his nonsense. If we were swapping out the barbecue for fine dining next year, I was going to make this last Summer BBQ Excursion the best there had ever been.

"From today, Jessie," he said, eyeing me seriously.

"What?" I could feel the furrows in my forehead as I glared down at him. "What do you mean, from today?"

"I mean, today we'll be serving a gourmet champagne brunch instead of barbecue chicken and burgers."

I gasped and fell heavily back into my seat.

"That's what they're all here for, Jessica," Walter said eagerly from his corner. I shot him a dark look.

"And no one thought to tell me this *before* we left the platform? I've got a fridge full of barbecue food, for goodness sake!"

"You're a clever thing, Jessie," Greg said with that smug grin again. "I'm sure you'll think of something."

"It's Jessica," I snapped. "And Penny is shucking a whole box of corn as we speak. What..." I scoffed in shock and outrage, looking down at the desk as though searching for an answer. "We've only got barbecue supplies, Greg. You've seen the size of my kitchen. It's not like we can keep supplies for every time you change your mind at the last minute!"

"Hey." Greg held his arms in the air and shrugged. "If you're really as good as you say you are, it won't be a problem, will it?"

He grinned at me, and I could feel myself beginning to seethe, my nostrils flaring. I had to get out of there—and I had to come up with a new menu, stat. I leapt up and swung around, yanking the door open.

"That's it," Greg said happily. "Back to work we go."

I didn't dare turn and say another word to him, because I knew it would not be a kindly word. I marched from the room, enraged by what he had done this time. It was as though he was purposely trying to trip me up. It wasn't even that I was particularly against the idea of a champagne brunch, but he could have at least told me before I'd prepped for a barbecue! And the way he talked about tourists as though they were gods drove me round the bend, as if the townsfolk —who were nothing if not loyal to us—were worthless.

I wasn't far down the corridor before I heard Walter's light foot-steps pattering behind me. He had a strangely small stride for a man, and it made him sound a little like a child.

"Jessica!"

I spun around. I was not in the mood. "What is it, Walter?"

He winced at my harsh tone and again and offered me an apologetic shrug. "It won't be as bad as you think. It may even work out nicely. I know you like a challenge."

I closed my eyes and sighed, pinching the bridge of my nose. Walter was a sweet guy, even if he was a little irritating at times. I hadn't meant to take my mood out on him.

"You're right, I'm sorry. I didn't mean to snap. It's just—"

"I get it, Jessica. It's all right."

"Well, I'd best get back to the kitchen," I said.

"All right. Catch you later."

Walter waved as he left, and I took a deep breath, nodding my goodbye. Then I turned and returned to my haven.

* * *

"That's another one who sends their compliments to the chef," Amy said as she walked backwards through the swinging door, a pile of dirty dishes balanced in her arms. "Reckon they've licked the plates clean!"

"Ew. That's gross," Penny replied, up to her elbows in suds as she scrubbed the saucepans clean. I wouldn't let them go in the dishwasher—my equipment was far too precious to risk having their protective coatings stripped off by a machine.

Amy shrugged as she put the dishes down and then began to stack them into the washer.

"They're getting washed anyway, so what does it matter?" Vanessa asked.

"As long as they enjoyed it," I said, eyeing each of them as I stirred the sauce on the stove.

"Said it was the best meal they'd had in ages," Amy said.

"Not surprising." Vanessa grinned. "Our Jessica's the best when it comes to cooking."

"Thanks, Ness," I said, looking fondly over at my friend.

"Smells good in here," Amy said as she closed the washer door. "What's cooking?"

"Blueberry pie," I said.

"Pie!" Vanessa raised an eyebrow. "Meeting with Greg really was that bad, was it?"

"Am I that easy to read?" I asked with a mock grimace.

"I'd say no, but I'd be lying," Vanessa said.

I laughed, then pulled the oven gloves from their hook on the wall and opened the oven door. I embraced the heat that immediately engulfed me, and the blueberry essence that swirled around in it. The latticed pastry was a golden brown, and from the gaps, the fruit bubbled enticingly.

I pulled it out, closed the door with my hip, and was about to put the pie onto the rack to cool. But the train lurched to a sudden stop, jolting us, and I dropped it. It landed upside down, a splatter of purple and blue spreading out across the floor.

All four of us froze to the spot, looking at each other in surprise. My heart began to race. This wasn't good. Whatever it was, it wasn't good.

"What the heck was that?" Penny asked.

"Language," I reminded her, raising an eyebrow. "And I have no idea."

"Something wrong with the engines?" Amy suggested with a shrug.

"Someone on the track!" Penny said with a giggle of nervous excitement.

"Don't be so gruesome," Vanessa said. "Signal stop, maybe?"

I looked out of the window to check where we were on the line. We had stopped on a bridge!

"Definitely not signals," I said, nodding out of the window at the valley below us.

"Oh."

The others looked as shaken up as I felt. There was *definitely* something wrong.

"Just . . . Amy, go out there and keep everyone calm, will you? Act like this is all perfectly normal, that it's a routine stop. I'll go find out what's happening. Vanessa, sit tight."

"What about me?" Penny asked as I was about to push the door open.

"You clean up that ruined pie, please."

The train was filled with questioning murmurs as I rushed through the carriages on my way to Greg's office.

"Jessica, dear, what's happening?"

"I don't know, Dorothy," I replied, smiling down at the sweet old lady who had put a hand out to stop me. "But I'm going to find out." She had become something of a regular of late, riding the rails for the sheer pleasure of watching the wildlife. Her hands were covered in heavy rings and she wore, as par for the course, a huge floppy hat that I was sure must get in the way sometimes. And, of course, she had binoculars hanging around her neck, and a book about birds always clutched in her hand.

"Well, do come back and tell us, won't you?"

"Of course," I said. "You'll be the first to know."

"This isn't a scheduled stop," Carter cried from across the way. "I demand to know what's going on."

"Oh, stop being such a grump," Dorothy replied, looking at him from over the top of her glasses.

Just then, we began to move again. I smiled as best I could. "You see, all fine," I said, then carried on down the aisle. They could argue it out amongst themselves. Still, I could feel the lump in my throat growing. I couldn't put her finger on *why* exactly, but I knew this unplanned stop was more than just a technical failure. When I finally got to Greg's office, he was talking animatedly with one of the engineers, so loudly that their voices could be heard from the corridor.

I pressed my ear against the door, but their words were too muffled. I grabbed hold of the knob and burst into the room, determined to know the truth. They both turned and looked at me, wide-eyed in horror.

"What is it?" I demanded. "What's happened? Why has the train stopped?"

"They've found a body, Jessica," Greg said, his face drained of color. "In the motorcar."

CHAPTER 4

"*A* body! But . . ." My jaw worked as I tried to find the words, but none came. This was far worse than even I'd imagined. "Whose body?"

"It's Walter, Jessica," the engineer said, twisting his cap in his hands. "Walter's been murdered."

Time seemed to freeze, and I felt myself pale. Did I hear them right? No, surely not. I let out a little unbelieving laugh and shook my head at them.

"What? What are you talking about?"

Even the fearful looks on their faces and their wide eyes weren't enough for me to believe it. Walter? Dead? But I only just saw him.

"He's telling the truth, Jessica," Greg said. "Someone has killed Walter."

"How? I mean, why? I . . . I don't understand."

I flopped into the same chair I had sat in earlier, trying to make sense of what they were saying. They were just words, weren't they? *Dead, murdered*. It was as though they didn't really mean anything in real life. And yet . . .

"Oh God, I can't believe this is happening," Greg said, running his hand over the top of his head.

His eyes were haunted, and if I didn't know any better, he was on the verge of tears. The atmosphere was so thick in that little room that you had to wade through it, like a soup of fear and dread and disbelief. I looked from Greg to Ralph and back to the floor, and it hit me in that moment. This was real and not some sort of sick joke.

Poor Walter. He never hurt a fly, just got on with his life without bothering anyone.

"But who could possibly want someone like Walter dead?" I asked, still in shock. All three of us looked to the floor or the desk or the walls, unable to make eye contact as we let this terrible thing sink in. "Walter is the last person who I would have thought had enemies."

"I don't know who or why, Jessica, only that it's true," Greg said. I could hear the exasperation in his tone. He was as clueless as I was.

He plonked himself down in the chair opposite me. He looked genuinely terrified in a way I'd never seen before, but then we'd never discovered a dead body before, either. He silently pleaded with me, his eyes begging me somehow. But for what? What did he want from me? To make it all go away? I couldn't do that anymore than he could.

"Looks like he's . . . er . . ." Ralph still twisted his cap and cleared his throat. "Looks like he was stabbed," he managed to say.

Ralph was a lanky man, maybe forty years old or so, and he had a long, drawn face. He always looked as though he had just seen the most terrible thing, habitually wide-eyed and frowning, despite his friendly nature. I supposed he had fair reason today as he stared at the floor, his brows heavily furrowed.

"Stabbed?" I repeated, letting out another choking laugh. It was then I remembered why I'd come here in the first place, and my head shot up to look at Greg. "Is that why the train stopped?"

"I stopped it as soon as I found the body," Ralph said. "But Greg sent word to restart it again."

I turned to look at Greg in absolute horror. "Why?" I asked, although in truth I didn't know whether it was better to stop or keep going. Walter's death surely deserved a little more ceremony that a few moments pause, but I also knew that stopping the train wouldn't bring him back.

Greg shrugged almost nonchalantly. "The show must go on," he said simply. "Speaking of which, Ralph, can you get back to the motorcar and please only tell those who need to know what is going on? Need to know basis, okay? No need to panic everyone. We've got to keep it as quite as possible—make sure they all know that! Tell them we're handling it as best we can, and that they must just continue to work as they always do."

Ralph shot me an uncertain glance but then nodded to Greg. "Whatever you say, boss," he said, then left the room.

Greg and I sat in silence for a long moment, neither of us quite sure what to say. I wanted to rail at him, to scream at him for wanting to continue as though nothing had happened. Did he really not care about *anything*? It seemed his precious profits were more important than the loss of a life, and that made me mad with fury. There was a man dead, a murderer on board the train, and he was worried about carrying on like normal!

I sat there shaking my head, these thoughts whirring around, until finally I looked up at him, aghast. "You can't be serious," I said.

"What do you want me to do, Jessica? We have to keep the train moving if we stop the killer could escape," he snapped, his hands gesticulating wildly as he spoke, his voice both higher and louder than usual. "We've got over a hundred people on this train, and we have a responsibility to keep them safe and happy. And wouldn't it be better if they left us feeling like they'd had a great day instead of being dragged into whatever is going on here? Or shall I gather them all together and tell them there's a dead body onboard and one of them is the killer? That's sure to keep chaos at bay, isn't it?"

I nodded and looked away, ashamed that I had so quickly thought badly of him. We had all the passengers to look after as well, and telling them what had happened would cause commotion. Greg wasn't being cruel when he said the show had to go on. He was just doing his best to keep everyone calm in a situation he had no experience in handling.

"You're right," I said softly, though without meeting his gaze. I always did hate admitting when I was wrong.

Poor, poor Walter. I'm not going to deny that there were times I wanted to throttle him, but he didn't deserve to be murdered. He was sweet and innocent. Irritating at times, admittedly, but he always tried his best and he wasn't a bad sort, not really. I leant back against the chair and let out another unbelieving sigh.

"Where is he now? Walter, I mean," I said.

Greg at least had the decency to look embarrassed this time as he met my gaze from the corner of his eyes. "He's still there. In the motorcar."

"You can't be serious?" I scoffed.

"We've only just found him, Jessica, and we didn't know what to do," Greg said.

"So, what, there's just a corpse lying on the ground?"

Greg winced. "We put a blanket over him. There's nothing much we can do until we get to the station."

"The infirmary?" I suggested, but Greg just shook his head.

"Not possible. What if someone needs to use it?"

"When was the last time someone used the infirmary?" I cried, not believing what I was hearing.

"Doesn't mean they won't this time, Jess, and we can't have anyone stumbling upon a dead computer analyst."

As loath as I was to admit it, Greg was right about that as well. Until we stopped and got help, we'd just have to ride it out.

"But you've contacted the authorities, right? I mean, they're meeting us at the next stop, aren't they?"

Greg winced again. "No."

I gasped and began frantically digging around in my pocket for my phone. The pockets of my jeans were tight, and my phone was big, so it often got jammed. And with the nervous horror that ran through my body, I didn't have the dexterity required to get it out. I growled in frustration.

"What are you doing?" Greg asked, somehow managing to look even more terrified than he had earlier.

"Getting my phone," I snapped. I thrust my hips in the air, straightening my body so I had better access to my pocket, and I fumbled. "What does it look like I'm doing?"

Phoning the police, obviously! Something you should have done already!"

I finally managed to pull the thing from my pocket, and it slipped from my fingers, bouncing to the floor. I reached down to grab it, but as I did so, Greg flew from his seat and snatched it before I had a chance.

"You can't call. I already tried. There's no cell signal," he said. His skin had turned so pale it was almost as white as snow. Even his lips had drained of color as he passed my phone back to me.

"We have to be able to find a signal. Aren't we going to pass a cell tower soon?" I asked in exasperation.

"As soon as we pass this mountain range, we should have something." He drummed his fingers on his desk. "I can't help but think that maybe in the meantime, we can solve it," he said, sitting back. "Me and you."

"What are you talking about now?" I asked, incredulous at what he was suggesting.

"Think about it, Jess."

"Jessica."

"Jessica. Sorry. I . . . We need to deal with this without anyone else knowing. We've still got two and a half hours until we reach our destination."

"With two stops before that," I reminded him.

"Come on, Jessica. You know as well as I do how remote those stations are. No network connection, unreliable cell service. It would take the authorities longer to get to those tiny little villages in the middle of nowhere than it would for us to get to the end of the line."

I clenched my jaw. That was true enough. I couldn't count the amount of times I'd stood in those little stations, willing my phone to find service if for nothing other than picking up my notifications. They really were remote places, not easily reached even from the road. Police would have trouble meeting us there at all.

"And seriously, what if stop and the killer just waltz off the train? I can't do that do poor Walter. He deserves justice." His lips straightened into a thin lip, and he paused. Then after a moment, he said, "Listen." He smiled sweetly at me.

Uh oh. I knew that expression.

It meant he wanted something from me.

"We'll call the police as soon as we have a signal but help me investigate while we're still on the move, that way we can hand the killer over to the authorities when they arrive."

"No," I said firmly. "I'm no investigator, Greg. I'm a chef!"

"And a wonderful one too," he said. I snarled at him. "I know how clever you are, Jessica, and I remember how much you love a good puzzle. Just think of it as that—a puzzle."

"It's not a puzzle though, is it, Greg? It's a man's life and a murderer."

"I know. It's serious. But we can work it out between us. It'll be easier while everyone is on the train rather than waiting for the cops to deal with it. Think of poor Walter."

"I said no, Greg. Absolutely not. I have absolutely no desire to get caught up in a murder investigation, no matter how badly I feel for Walter. Besides, I've got my own problems to deal with."

"Such as?" he asked, raising an eyebrow at me.

I got up from my seat and looked down at him. "Such as turning barbecue food into fine dining!"

I turned and stormed out, not listening to his shouts calling me back. If he really wanted to do this, he would have to do it on his own. I wanted no part in it. Besides, I wasn't lying. I already had a challenge on my hands, especially if Greg insisted on carrying on as normal.

I heard the door slam shut behind me and I paused for a moment, slowing my breath and letting everything else catch up to me. That's when she popped up from around the corner. Beverly Lyonel, the winemaker.

"Ah, there you are, Jessica."

"Not now, Mrs. Lyonel," I snapped, and I stormed past her, the low heels on my shoes clipping loudly on the floor.

"But—"

"Not now!" But that's when a thought came to me, and I spun back around. "You were surprised when I said I was cooking barbecue food."

"Well, yes," she said, blinking at me. "The ticket stated a champagne—"

"Actually, what are you even doing in this part of the train? It's for staff only."

"Yes," she said again, visibly flustered now as she took a step backward. "I . . . I . . . I just wanted someone to . . . well, answer my questions."

I looked at her blankly for a moment, then said, "Return to your coach, Mrs. Lyonel. I'll come find you when I have time."

What was Mrs. Lyonel *really* doing in this part of the train?

CHAPTER 5

*A*s I walked back through the train, I felt numb with shock. Walter was dead! And to make things worse, his killer was somewhere on this train. Everything sounded so loud within my mind: the laughter of the passengers, the repetitive sounds of the wheels going over the tracks. I had to stop more than once to force myself to breathe. All I could think about was Walter and who could have done such a thing to him. My mind raced through all the staff, then all the passengers, and no one stood out as capable.

"Ms. Preston, isn't it?" I turned to look at the man in question—smartly dressed, clean shaven, tall. A woman simpered behind him—his wife, I presumed.

"Yes, who is asking?"

"Mr. Wallis," he said. "And this is my wife. We saw your photograph in the brochure."

"I see. How can I help you?"

I couldn't for the life of me work out what this man wanted with me, not when there was a dead body onboard. He seemed so cheerful, like he didn't care.

"We had a bite to eat earlier on—keep us going until the brunch, you know how it is." He chuckled, and I frowned at him. "We just wanted to say how wonderful it was. We really must congratulate you on producing such wonderful food—and on a train, too!"

"I don't know how you do it," Mrs. Wallis said over his shoulder.

"Oh, well, thank you," I said with a smile. Of course, they didn't know about Walter, did they? I felt myself blush—something I *never* did and I don't know why I did then, but my cheeks were definitely burning. "I must be getting back," I said politely. "Lots to prepare."

I turned and walked quickly down the aisle, widening my eyes at my own foolishness. What was wrong with me? *Walter's dead*, that voice inside me cried. Oh yeah, that.

Just focus on getting dinner ready, Jessica. It'll all be over soon.

My cheeks were still burning, and I hoped they weren't glowing as red as they felt. I looked around me suspiciously, convinced everyone was watching me, staring at me, knew what I was thinking. They *were* watching me, of course. I was striding down the middle of the train looking like someone had died, while they sat back and enjoyed the view.

Get it together, Jessica!

The train shuddered then, and I stumbled. Luckily, I was already at the end of the first coach, and I grabbed hold of the rail to stop myself from falling. I considered going back, finding out what happened this time, but I reminded myself trains do that sometimes, and that I was being overly paranoid. I went through the join and into the next coach.

"Ah, there you are," Carter said, leaping out of his seat as soon as the door closed behind me.

"Carter," I said, smiling weakly.

"Well? What was the problem?" he asked.

"I . . . oh, it was . . . a . . . technical . . . error," I stuttered, then shook my head, annoyed at myself. I couldn't very well tell the truth—Greg had been right about that—but what was I supposed to say? I chuckled to disguise my irritation. "You know me, Carter. No idea about the engineering side of things. I can prepare the fanciest meal you can imagine, but ask me anything about steam engines and . . ." I trailed off, seeing from his confused expression that I was talking far too much.

"Do they need assistance?" he asked. "As you know, I've long studied steam engines. I am quite *au fait* when it comes to these things." He grinned proudly. "I even wrote a book about them once."

"Did you actually finish that one?" Dorothy asked.

"Well . . . I . . ." Poor old Carter looked flustered, so I jumped in to save him from embarrassment.

"No, that's a kind offer, but they've got it under control now," I said, offering him the best smile I could muster.

"Are you sure?" he asked. He made as if to move down the train. "Perhaps I could just—"

"No!" I said, far too quickly and a little louder than strictly necessary. "I mean, it's fine, it's all sorted. But they know where you are if they need you."

"Very well," he replied with a frown and sat himself back down.

"Are you all right, my dear?" Dorothy asked. "You seem a little flustered."

She, at least, stayed in her seat, only putting a hand out to mine. Her skin was like soft leather, wrinkled but supple from years of applying hand cream. Mine would never get like that, no matter how old I lived to be, not with my hands so often in water, thanks to my profession.

"I'm fine, Dorothy, thank you for asking. I have a lot to do, that's all. What with the brunch and all."

"Oh yes." She beamed, her eyes sparkling. "Dear Walter told me about the change of plan. He's a sweet boy, isn't he? Although I must say, I'm not overly happy about the change. Everybody loves the barbecue so much. I don't know why they would want to go messing around with something that has worked for so many years! Champagne brunch indeed."

I caught my breath, swallowed back the words that almost flew from my mouth. I nodded, tight-lipped, instead, then extracted my hand from hers and near enough ran to the restaurant cars. It was quiet when I got there, the early birds already fed and the restaurant now closed so we could prepare for the barbecue . . . or rather, the champagne brunch.

I sighed with relief at the quiet. I needed time to think, to let the news settle. I also had to work out what I was going to serve for dinner, and where I was going to get a few more cases of champagne. I knew there were a few bottles stashed away for special occasions, but nowhere near enough for all these people.

"What happened?" Amy said as she came through the door at the other end.

She had a box of silver cutlery held against her hip and she traversed the tables with practiced ease, carefully placing each set in an exact spot, lining them up so they matched. She had incredible attention to detail seemingly without even trying. It was one of the reasons I hired her in the first place.

I still hadn't answered, and she looked back up at me. "Jessica? Is everything all right? You look awful pale."

I nodded toward the kitchen door, indicating that she should follow me. She slowly put the box of cutlery on the table and followed, looking worried.

"So, if you think about it, it's unlikely to be a single thief." I heard Vanessa's voice even before I walked through the door, and I smiled, glad that, of all days, I had persuaded her to come along today.

I swung the door open.

"I don't get the big deal," Penny said, throwing the last of my beautiful pie into the bin. "I mean, it's just a fancy thumbtack, really."

She'd used reams and reams of paper towel, now soaked purple and blooming out of the bin. I'd have to remind her about waste.

"Did you hear that, Jessica?" Vanessa turned to me, eyebrows a good half an inch higher than where they should be, before turning back to Penny. "Apart from the fact that it's worth an absolute fortune," she said, elongating the word *fortune*, "it's a part of our history! Really, you kids today, no respect for the past."

"All right, both of you," I said, my voice low.

"Oh dear," Vanessa said. "What's that Greg done now? Funny how you always come back from his office with a face like thunder."

"It's not Greg," I said, not meeting her eye, even though I could feel hers on me.

I walked to the far end of the kitchen, guiding myself with my hand on the countertop, as though I couldn't trust my legs to hold me up, until I reached the stools. I sank down next to Vanessa and stared at the floor, feeling the tension in the air around me. The three of them had stopped stock-still, and when their eyes weren't bearing down on me, they were looking at each other questioningly, silently asking each other what they should do.

"Jessica?" Vanessa finally asked, putting a hand on my knee and ducking her head to catch my eye. "What's happened?"

I looked up at them, not quite sure I could get the words out, but after a moment's pause, they came tumbling from my mouth in rapid succession.

"Walter's dead. His body was found in the motorcar. It seems he's been stabbed, and the killer must be onboard because they haven't had a chance to get off, and Greg can't reach the authorities since we don't have any service and we've still got hours to go. There's nothing we can do until we're at the station. And he doesn't want to cause a panic, and he's right, so we're trying to keep it a secret, and we want to keep everyone happy and safe at the same time. And I've got to find some way of turning barbecue sauce into au jus fit for a champagne brunch and—"

"Jessica, Jessica!" Vanessa said, taking my hand and clutching it. "Slow down!"

I looked up at her, my brow furrowed and my jaw working, but no more words coming out.

"Walter's dead?" Amy asked, slowly leaning against the countertop. "Murdered?"

"Yes," I said.

"All right." Vanessa's calm voice washed over me. She always was good in other people's stressful situations. Her own she was not so good at, but whenever I needed reassuring or comforting, she was there. "Start at the beginning, and slower this time. Who's Walter?"

"Computer tech," Amy said, answering for me. "Or, he was."

"I watched a film just like this, once," Penny said excitedly. "Someone was murdered on a train, and then there was a race to catch the killer before he struck again."

"Wow, thanks," I said, looking blankly back at her. "That's helpful, yeah."

36

"Sorry," she replied, looking a little sheepish.

I told them the whole story then, from the moment I left the kitchen to the moment I returned. They stopped me here and there to ask questions—most of which I didn't have the answers to—but otherwise, they listened intently, like I was spinning a yarn.

"I know how crazy this sounds, but it really made me look at everyone differently, including our regulars. Even poor old Dorothy!"

"No, Dorothy wouldn't," Amy said. "Would she?"

"Of course not," I said, rolling my eyes at her. "But it's got to be one of them, hasn't it?"

"First a museum heist and now a murder," Vanessa said. "Whoever thought Golden could be this exciting?"

"Exciting! Hardly appropriate, Vanessa! And anyway," I said, slapping my hands on my thighs to signal the end of the conversation, then getting up from my seat. "We've got to get on. Regardless of what's happened, we've still got over a hundred people to feed and we still have no idea what they'll be eating!"

"What do you mean?" Vanessa looked at me as though I'd gone quite mad, and she, too, jumped from her stool. "You're not going to take Greg up on his offer then?"

"What offer?" I asked. She rolled her eyes.

"To help out with the investigation! That is what you just said, isn't it?"

"Yeah, that what I said, but no," I said firmly. "I most definitely am *not* going to do it."

I frowned deeply at her, exaggerating my expression to both make her laugh and see how serious I was being. It worked, because she held her hands in the air and sat back down.

"All right, all right," she said. "Whatever you say. I suppose we can only solve one crime at a time anyway."

"Ah yes, the heist," I said, hoping to take my mind off the murder. "Do we have any more theories on that front yet?"

I let the three of them chatter on in the background, not really listening as I pulled ingredients out of the chiller. We didn't have a lot. With the space we had, I tended to restock for each journey, meaning that other than a few kitchen staples, I only had barbecue food to deal with. I sighed for what felt like the millionth time that day, deciding that the only thing I could do was elevate the barbecue, somehow.

Present it better, maybe.

There was a stop coming up too. It was a tiny little village, just somewhere for people to stretch their legs really and admire their surroundings. But there was a small market, and I'd half hoped I could jump off the train and grab a few more supplies. But now, Greg was never going to let that happen.

And he was right. No reason to stop and let someone get away with murder...

I sighed.

It would have been nice if the store had some salmon steaks and a little brie, even a pot of cream would have helped.

"But it makes sense it being a woman, if you think about it," Penny said.

"How so?" Vanessa asked.

"Small enough to squeeze in and out of windows, for a start," Penny explained.

"Small men do exist, you know, Penny," Amy said dryly. "I don't think we can count size as a factor in determining gender."

"And what does it matter, anyway?" Vanessa asked. "Whoever stole the spike had to have ..."

I tuned out again as I slapped my raw chicken breasts down onto the chopping board and began to slice through them, trimming off the edges. The task was monotonous, and one I would normally assign to Penny, but she hadn't finished with the corn, and I found it therapeutic. It meant I didn't have to concentrate too much, and I could let my mind wander.

The question was still going around in my head.

Why would anyone want to kill Walter?

He wasn't rich, so it couldn't have been for money. I couldn't imagine he had ever got in a fight with anyone or caused trouble, and I was pretty sure he was single, so it couldn't have been relationship troubles. The motive for his murder was the most baffling bit of the whole thing, unless Walter had a secret life none of us knew about, of course.

38

I shook my head, forcing the thoughts away. I would *not* let my intrigue run away with me. I would *not* get involved in this investigation. I had to focus on what I was doing, and that alone.

"Maybe it hasn't been stolen at all," Penny said. "Maybe it's just been hidden."

"And why on earth would anybody want to do that?" Vanessa said, shaking her head at Penny. She'd pulled an orange from her pocket and was peeling it, throwing her waste into the bowl at her side. She always had some kind of snack in her pocket. She liked to be prepared.

"So that they can go back and collect it later, when all the interest has died down," Amy said. "That's not a bad theory actually, Penny."

"You girls talk some nonsense," Vanessa said. "Anyway, the heist is old news. We should be talking about murder now." She widened her eyes on the word *murder*, and I let my knife clatter to the counter before turning to look at her.

"No, we shouldn't," I said. "The heist is fair game, but what's happened today is entirely different. A man has lost his life—it's not entertainment! Let the relevant authorities deal with it. There's nothing we can do."

Vanessa opened her mouth to answer, but before she could, Greg burst through the kitchen door. He looked just as haunted and desperate as he had in his office, but I wouldn't let him pull at my sympathies. I *would not* get involved, no matter how much he tried to sweet-talk me into it.

"Jessica, a word, please."

"What is it, Greg?" I asked. I looked down and realized I held my chef's knife in midair, the tip of it glinting in the light. I gasped, realizing just how threatening it must look, and placed it gently on the chopping board.

"In private," he said.

"Whatever you want to say to me, you can say in front of my team," I said simply.

He looked reluctant, his glance skirting over Penny, Amy, and finally Vanessa. But then, with a sigh, he nodded. "Fine."

CHAPTER 6

"All right," Greg said. "I take it everyone knows what's happened."

Amy and Penny focused their attentions elsewhere, suddenly fascinated by their work in the way they always were when Greg came into the room. But Vanessa nodded to him, eager to know what he was going to say.

"I've explained everything," I said, trying my best to keep the emotion from my voice.

"Right. Good," he said with a weak smile, then shook his head. "Not good, but . . ."

"I know what you mean," I said, seeing the confusion and loss in his eyes.

He was stressed, that was plain to see. If he wasn't running his hands through his now-messy hair, he was worrying with his fingers, twisting them around each other. He seemed to have aged a year in just the short journey we'd taken today, and his eyes had dark black circles beneath them. It was quite something, how quickly a man could go from smart and fresh to this near wreck.

Death does funny things to people.

"Please help me," he said. "I can't reach the authorities. I asked Lucas to use the office radio but so far, he's gotten no response. He's going to keep trying, but we need to ensure no one else gets hurt, and I don't know where to start. Your help would mean the world to me."

"I told you already, Greg. I'm no investigator, and I really don't want to get involved."

"But you're so good when it comes to these sorts of things," he said.

"These sorts of things?" I repeated, letting out an unbelieving laugh. He couldn't be serious! "Remind me again. When *was* the last time we investigated a murder together?" I put my finger to my lips in mock thought and glared at him, but I instantly regretted it. He looked broken.

"Mysteries, I meant. Puzzles. Dilemmas. You're good at figuring things out, unlike me. It's one of the main reasons I hired you!"

I could feel Vanessa gawking at us both, her head bobbing back at forth like she was watching a tennis match. Amy and Penny, though listening intently, so studiously avoided looking at us it was almost comical. I would have chuckled, except I was worried that would lead to tears. I was a tough cookie, I knew that well enough, but death always got to me, and I hated the idea of anyone I knew dying. I had to keep it inside, at least until we got off this train.

"I would hardly put the Sunday crossword and a murder investigation in the same category, Greg!" I said. "This needs to be handled properly. Why can't you see that?"

"I can see that," he insisted. "But there's more than two hours until we can get help; we don't have a lot of choice. It's not just about finding out who the culprit is, but also stopping it from happening again without causing a mass panic. Will you help me, please?"

"No," I replied, even firmer this time.

Greg fell back against the countertop, making it thump with his weight, and I'm sure he let out a little whimper. He buried his face in his hands and groaned.

"This was never meant to happen," he said into his hands, his words muffled. "Not on my watch. I don't know what to do."

I stared at him for a moment, then asked, "What's really going on, Greg? This is not like you. You can normally handle any situation. There must be more to this than Walter's death."

There was a long, tense pause, his answer hanging in the thick air before he finally spoke, still through the gaps in his fingers. "What if they blame me?" he muttered.

"What?!" Vanessa and I cried the word at exactly the same time, shooting each other a look before turning back to Greg.

"Why would they blame *you*?" I asked, confused.

He let his hands drop down to his thighs and sighed. "Because . . . because I have motive, I suppose."

I couldn't stop myself from rolling my eyes. He was being dramatic. "Greg, being train manager doesn't automatically put you in the firing line for accusations."

I laughed; the very thought of Greg as a suspect was ridiculous. But he went as pale as he had in his office, and he looked at me with those pleading eyes again. I stopped laughing, the smile slipping from my face.

"What have you done, Greg?" I asked, my tone giving him as much a warning as my words.

"I think you'd best come and sit down," Vanessa said, glaring at him as she patted the stool next to her. "And start telling us everything —from beginning to end."

He nodded meekly and followed her instructions, sitting down so carefully it looked as though he might snap. He said nothing for a long while, all four of us staring at him now, waiting for his explanation.

"Well?" I demanded eventually, my hip against the counter and my arms crossed over my chest.

"I . . . well, the thing is, Walter made quite a big error, and one he admitted to me just before our meeting."

"I thought he was Mr. Wonderful after doubling sales with this champagne brunch you're making Jessica do," Vanessa said, butting in.

"Yeah," I added. "That's certainly the impression I got."

There was that sheepish, embarrassed look again, the one where he avoided meeting anyone's gaze, his cheeks flushing the gentlest of pinks.

"About that," he said, not looking at me. "I'm sorry for the way I spoke to you in my office, Jessica. I was out of order."

I sighed, neither accepting nor rejecting his apology. "What happened?" I asked.

"Walter did double ticket sales with the champagne brunch idea, and that was great. Except . . ." Greg paused, openmouthed, looking from me to Vanessa and back again. "Except he also accidentally put out a free brunch promo at the same time. So, while ticket sales went up, revenue has gone down, and by quite a margin. I'm not even sure we'll break even on this trip."

"And you were angry at Walter for that," Vanessa said, nodding her understanding.

"Yes, I was," Greg said quickly. "If we don't pull a profit, the train gets shut down. It's that simple. No train, no job for me, you, the engineers . . . Everyone here is out of a job! Not to mention the tourism Golden pulls in . . . Even Vanessa would be effected."

Vanessa gave him a sharp look.

"But I didn't kill him!" Greg continued, ignoring Vanessa. "God, Jessie, you do believe me, don't you?"

"I would if you started calling me by my proper name," I snorted.

But of course, I believed him. Greg was no killer. A fool perhaps, but never a murderer.

"Yes, sorry." He shook his head. "And again, I'm really sorry about being so brash in our meeting. I was trying to save face and—"

"You were trying to push your problems onto me, you mean," I snapped a little unfairly. "Seriously, Greg. Walter gets you into trouble, and not only do you expect me to sort it out, but you act like I'm the one causing problems when I complain about it!"

"I know, I know," he said quickly, his hands tapping down the air as if to calm me. "You're absolutely right. But you've got to understand how stressed I've been, Jessica."

"Oh, Greg," I sighed. I rubbed my temples with my fingers, closing my eyes for a moment and trying to block everything out. Today was not turning out anything like I had expected.

"So, does that mean you'll help?" he asked hopefully.

I didn't open my eyes or turn to look at him. I just shook my head and said, "No." I couldn't help, no matter how intrigued I was by the events of the morning. I really, really didn't want to get involved. I was a chef, not a police chief. I thought back to those who had accosted me on my way back from the office—Dorothy, Carter, that winemaker from Napa, Mrs. Lyonel. There was that couple too. And the woman who seemed not to be enjoying herself at all.

It could have been any one of them.

Or, more likely, I thought, it was somebody lying low, hiding themselves away. The killer wouldn't make themselves stand out from the crowd by starting conversations, would they? Surely they'd want to make themselves as inconspicuous as possible. But not necessarily. What was that old saying?

Hide in plain sight?

It was just as likely that our killer would make him or herself known with the express intention of making us *believe* they couldn't possibly have done it.

So many possibilities!

I furrowed my brow and stared out of the window as we trundled through the forest. Such a beautiful sight. Even though I did this trip every day, it never failed to capture my attention. The rich greens and shades of brown were enough, but the rays of sunshine that broke through the gaps and bore down onto the earth made it look magical.

Every now and then, you'd see a bird dip and swoop as they flew from tree to tree. Dorothy and I had talked about it often—she knew everything anyone could know about birds, and she loved it if anyone got her on the topic. I always liked to imagine them visiting a neighbor, as if they lived in little communities, or delivering food to their young. It was the hovering hummingbirds I liked best, though, like fairies dancing in the air. Ever since I was a child, I'd been fascinated by them, and I loved catching a glimpse of their brightly colored feathers through the trees. How could someone commit murder in such majestic surroundings?

I sighed and turned back to my companions. "I suppose we'd best get on with elevating this meal to something worthy of a champagne brunch," I said.

I picked the chopping board up and slid the prepared chicken into a plastic tub, ready to be cooked later, then threw the waste into the waste pot, for compost. I stirred the barbecue sauce that sat on the stove cooling, then cleaned down my station and pulled out the beans. I'd already decided I'd add Worcestershire sauce and brown sugar to them to give them something more than your standard barbecue beans. And I could serve them in little ramekins on the side of the plate, a bit of parsley sprinkled on top. I had miniature sauce boats to serve the sauce in too, giving the whole thing a bit of a classier look.

Greg's eyes were on me. I could feel them as strongly as if they were burning through me, but I avoided his gaze.

"How about a deal?" he said eventually.

"A deal?" I side-eyed him but with an eyebrow raised, hoping a double-whammy of disapproving looks would persuade him to give this up.

"You help me find out what happened, and I'll let you serve the barbecue fare you'd planned all along."

"I beg your pardon?" I scoffed at his sheer audacity! I wouldn't be bought, not for any price. And if he wanted a gourmet feast, then a gourmet feast was what he would receive.

"That way, we both get what we want," he said, throwing me an uncertain smile.

I would have thought even Greg knew what a bad move that would be, trying to trade with me, as if I couldn't live up to the first challenge he set me. I didn't say anything for a while, but I did bang around the kitchen, thinking through all the things I still had to do— including working out what to do with the chicken and making fresh pies from scratch!

But then I turned and railed on him, outraged at his suggestion.

"You asked me to change the menu, Greg. You, no one else. *You* told me it was what the customers wanted. Well, that's what you're going to get. I'm a classically trained chef, and I will rise to this challenge. You should try and have a little more faith in me."

"I do have faith in you," he said quickly. "But we're also running out of time!"

"Exactly!" I snapped, whipping around to glare at him. "And I have a lot of work to do, so if you don't mind . . ."

"Actually . . ."

I turned to look at Vanessa in surprise. I'd almost forgotten she was there, which is a first with her. She's not normally one to stay so quiet.

"Actually what?" I asked.

She got up from her seat and joined me by the counter, where she rubbed my arm companionably.

"Actually, I think Greg is right—and not just because I'd prefer a burger and fries over some fancy-pants meal."

I frowned at her, wanting to argue. But there's no way Vanessa would pick Greg's side over mine unless she genuinely thought it was for the best. She always sided with me, except when she thought I was wrong, and that's what made her such a good friend.

"It's the right thing to do, Jessica," she said, looking me straight in the eyes.

"I agree," Amy piped up from behind me.

"Me too," Penny added.

I glanced over to Greg. He had the strangest mix of defeat and victory written over his face, although perhaps exhaustion and fear combined with relief that he had people on his side was more likely.

"Hey, what have we got to lose?" Vanessa asked, sounding almost excited. "We'll just ask a few questions, talk to some of the passengers. See what we can find out. Might even be fun!"

I sighed again, aware of how grating that sound was becoming, and I looked back at the four eager faces staring at me.

"I'll help, but only if you phone the police as soon as you can and tell them to meet us at the station. Whatever else you tell them is up to you, but make sure there is someone to greet us."

"Of course," Greg agreed.

"Okay then, I'll help," I said reluctantly. "But first, we have to get everything prepped for dinner."

CHAPTER 7

Once I had agreed, it was as though everyone kicked into action. All four of them huddled around me eagerly, looking at me as though I was in charge and somehow knew what to do. Why was it that every time something went wrong, it was down to me to find a way of fixing it? I supposed it was a compliment—they had faith in me, even when it came to murder.

"We should stop the train," Vanessa said, looking from me to Greg and back.

That had been my first thought too. But now it didn't make much sense to me. We had no assistance, and if we stopped in the middle of nowhere, I worried the authorities wouldn't make it to us at all—or, if they did, it would take them a long time.

"No, we need to keep going," I said. "If we stop the train, everyone will know something is going on. How will we keep everyone calm then?"

Greg looked at me incredulously, and I could hardly blame him. I'd done a complete about-turn, arguing what he argued back in his office. I'd wanted the train to be stopped then; it seemed completely insane and heartless to carry on. But I wasn't so stubborn that I couldn't listen, and Greg had made a good case for continuing on the journey. Now, after more thought, it made perfect sense, and the sooner we got to the station—and to the cops—the better.

"We'll say it's engine troubles or something," Vanessa said, shrugging.

"Good idea," Amy added. "There's no need for them to know anything about Walter. We can make something up so it's less scary."

"That way, nobody will be able to get on or off," Vanessa said, eager now she had support. "And we'll know whoever did it is still amongst our midst."

"And we'll be trapped on a train with a murderer," I muttered. "That's what I'm worried about."

I wasn't worried, not really. Not for myself, at least, and not truly for anyone else. I figured that if someone was on a murderous rampage, killing just for the sake of it, we'd have seen more action by now or at least someone acting strangely. No, it was much more likely that Walter was killed for a reason, that he was singled out. We just needed to work out what that reason was—finding motive would surely lead us to the perpetrator.

"What do you think, Greg?" Vanessa asked.

We all looked at him. Some of the color had returned to his cheeks and he had less of the disturbed look about him. Having someone to share the burden of all this was obviously doing him good. Great—we'd achieved something, at least.

"We need to prevent people from coming and going," he said simply. "Listen, nobody outside us know anything about this, and that's the way it should stay. We need to keep it contained."

I turned away from the group and went to the chiller, pulling out packs of bacon and letting them fall onto the countertop with a slap.

"Penny, you start peeling the potatoes," I said, nodding over to where we kept the vegetables caged up to prevent them from rolling around with the movement of the train. "We're going to sauté them with some shallots instead of serving fries. Amy, I want you to get all that corn off the cobs, please. Give it a wash, then into a pan. We'll have sweetcorn soup as an appetizer."

"You don't have to do this, Jess," Greg said. "Burgers and grilled corn sound great."

I turned and scowled at him. "These people came on this trip expecting gourmet. Now, I can't do magic, and if I'd been given a bit more warning, things would be very different. But I'll tell you this for certain: murder or no murder, stop the train or not, I'm serving them a meal that is as elevated as I can possibly make it with what poor supplies I've got. And it's Jessica! Understood?"

He leaned further back against the counter as if trying to get away from me and nodded, while Vanessa and the others chuckled in the background. "Yeah, all right, point taken."

"You don't set our Jessica a challenge and not expect her to complete it," Vanessa said, cocking her head to one side. Her whole body shook as she laughed. "Would have thought you knew that by now, Greg."

"Yeah," he said, relaxing and staring at me with a broad smile. "I'm starting to learn just how determined she can be."

"You're the one who said the show must go on," I muttered under my breath, but he obviously heard it.

"I did, and you're right. We'll keep the train going for now, with the option of stopping it later if need be."

Thoughts of the market and being able to purchase salmon, brie and cream jumped to mind.

"Thank you," I said quietly.

He was still staring at me, and I shifted uncomfortably under his gaze, not quite looking at him. He had a twinkle in his eye, almost like he was enjoying this—but whether *this* was the investigation or the fact that he was working with me was not certain. That smile was like one you gave a lover, not an employee or even a friend.

I slid the meat board down from the shelf, then cut open the packs of bacon and laid the slices out on the board, focusing as much of my attention on that as I could, all the while feeling Greg's hungry eyes on me.

"Hey, Vanessa," I said, looking sideways at her. "If you want to help, perhaps you could grab some more blueberries and give them a wash for me? You know, since my first pie went in the bin."

"You're making another pie?" Amy asked. She sounded surprised, and I knew why—time was running short, and we still had so much to do.

"There's some ready-made individual tart cases in the cupboard," I said, nodding my head in the direction of the storage. "Not ideal, and you know how much I hate not making stuff from scratch, but they're going to want dessert, and this is a quick and simple solution and there's enough for everyone."

"I knew you could do it, see?" Greg said, still smiling at me.

"Er . . . yeah," I said, squirming again. *What's got into him?*

I shot a glance at Vanessa who, with a big grin, nodded at the back of Greg's head. I rolled my eyes, and she mouthed the words *he's mooning over you.*

After laying four slices of bacon out, I took a chicken breast from the pot and rolled it up, placing it on a catering-sized baking sheet before beginning the next. I'd originally planned to do barbecue chicken skewers, but food on a stick is hardly fine dining.

Vanessa saw what I was doing and nodded approvingly. "What about the burgers?" she asked. "You were doing burgers, right?"

"Still am," I said with a shrug. "Brioche bun, cheese, shredded lettuce, tomato. Maybe we can caramelize some onions to put in there too and make a barbecue glaze sauce with fresh thyme. Don't know what else I can do with them to make them *gourmet*."

"So, what do you want me to do?" Greg asked, and I looked up at him aghast.

"You're the manager, Greg. Manage!"

"We should come up with some sort of plan," Vanessa said.

She tipped the remaining blueberries into a large colander, then waddled over to the sink. It felt good to have a busy kitchen, and I felt blessed to have such a team, even if Vanessa was only a temp. My hands were still busy with the meat, and I was grateful to have something to focus on. But Vanessa was right. If we were going to investigate this murder, we needed some sort of plan of action. We had to divide the tasks between us, then reconvene to discuss what we'd discovered. With over a hundred passengers and staff, there had to be someone who had seen something or who had some idea what the motive could have been.

"Our main goal is to find the killer. Agreed?" Everyone nodded. I had their attention again. "But we need to break that down. What other answers will lead us to that one? Motive, for one."

"Maybe how Walter was acting before he died?" Penny suggested, waving the potato peeler in the air. "Like, if he was angry or suspicious or something."

"Good thinking, Penny," I said. "What else?"

"Whether he knew anyone personally on the train," Vanessa said.

"We already know some of those, like the regulars, but yes, finding out who else he knew would be handy."

"There's the crime scene too," Greg said. "We've got to be careful not to disturb it, obviously, but I suppose we ought to check for clues. You know, like a hair or something. That's what they do in films, isn't it?"

"Ah, yeah." Vanessa gazed wistfully out of the window, her hand still in the colander as the water poured over the blueberries. "Columbo was always the best at that." She turned and grinned. "If he was here now, we'd have no worries at all."

"But he's not," I said, eyeing her.

"Who's Columbo?" Penny asked.

"Don't worry," I said. "Before your time. And also not at all relevant!"

I shot both Greg and Vanessa a look. If we were going to do this, then we had to take it seriously.

"No looking for stray hairs, then?" Greg asked, his nose crinkled in that *I'm being silly but I want you to play along* kind of way.

"No, but checking out the motorcar for clues is not a bad idea," I said.

"I can do that," Vanessa replied.

"But there's a dead body in there!" Amy cried, aghast at the very thought.

Vanessa shrugged. "I've never really been squeamish, and I reckon I've got a good eye for detail. Besides, it makes more sense that you guys talk to the passengers—you know them, and you have good reason for talking to them. You know, checking how their day is going and that sort of thing. I'm just a stranger to them; it'll be too weird for me to do that. I mean, I can strike up a conversation with one or two of them but . . ."

"You're right, Ness," I said, impressed she had thought of that. "Good thinking."

"How much champagne have we got?" Greg asked.

"Champagne!" Penny cried. "I didn't think this was a celebration."

"Not for me, you donut," Greg replied. "For the passengers."

"There's a case or two, but not a lot," Amy said. "I checked earlier when Jessica said we're doing a champagne brunch."

"I've got an idea," I said. "There's juice, isn't there?"

Amy put down her corn and went to check. She was nodding before she even closed the door. "Yep, loads of it."

"We'll make mimosas, then," I said, grinning to myself for thinking of such a good solution. "It'll make the champagne go a lot further."

"You're a genius!" Greg cried.

"I know," I said with a nonchalant shrug and a laugh. "So here's the plan. Vanessa, you check out the motorcar, and maybe you can talk to some of the engineers down there, see if they saw or heard anything."

"Got it," she said, shaking the colander of excess water then putting it down on the draining board.

"Greg, you go out there and liaise with the passengers. Just pretend you're doing your normal rounds, checking everyone is happy and enjoying themselves. Find out what people know, see if any of them are acting strange. If it seems natural, ask about Walter, but don't make it obvious."

"All right," he said. "I think I can manage that. Especially if I have one of those mimosas."

He winked, and I rolled my eyes. "We've hardly got enough to go around as it is," I warned.

"It'll look odd if I don't have at least one glass," he said, grinning at me. "They'll wonder what's wrong with me."

I groaned and shook my head. "Fine," I said. "But only one, got it?" General manager he may have been, but when it came to the kitchen, I was in charge.

"Got it," he said, nodding seriously. "I'll make it last."

"Amy, once we've got these mimosas made, you can hand them out and get people settled in the restaurant when the time comes. Again, keep an eye out, listen to conversations, maybe talk to people if it seems right."

"Will do," she replied.

"I'll get the rest of this prepped and cooking and set Penny on the right track, then I'll get out there and talk to people too. If this morning is anything to go by, there are lots of talkative people on board today."

"Mrs. Lyonel?" Vanessa asked, laughing at the memory of us being accosted on our way in.

"And the rest," I said.

"This shouldn't be too difficult then, should it?" Greg said.

"Sure," I said, shaking my head at him. "That's why homicides are so easily solved every single day."

"But we have an advantage," he said, cocking his head. "We've got everyone trapped."

He was such an idiot sometimes. I laughed despite myself. "For now," I said, raising an eyebrow to remind him that the train would keep moving, and we would arrive at the station eventually.

"For now is all we need," he said.

"So, we'll meet back here when we're done and discuss our findings?" Amy said.

"Yes," I said. "And remember—don't tell anyone about Walter. Our questioning should be subtle. We don't want to cause panic and pandemonium."

"Everyone ready then?" Greg asked.

"Wait a second," Vanessa said, holding her finger in the air. "If you're going out there with a mimosa, Greg, who's going to run the train?"

Greg shrugged. "There's not a whole lot to do on a train, to be honest," he said. "The engineers will keep us moving and keep an eye on the track ahead of us. As for anything else, my intern will deal with it."

"Intern? I didn't know you had an intern."

"You don't need to know everything about me, Jessie," he said, again with a grin. "I have some secrets."

"Jessica," I said ignoring his flirty smile.

"You mean Lucas?" Penny asked.

I spun around and blinked at her. How did she know the intern when I didn't?

"You two know each other?" Greg asked.

Penny shrugged, but her cheeks flushed a bright pink. Ah, that's why she knew him—she had a thing for him. "Met him once or twice," she mumbled, looking intently at the bowl of potato peelings in front of her.

"He's a nice young lad," Greg said. "A bit naïve, bit wet sometimes. But he's clever enough. He's perfectly capable of making sure the train stays on the track and stops where it's supposed to stop."

"Okay, it's agreed, then," I said, looking at each and every one of them seriously. "Remember: stay safe, don't give yourself away, and don't put yourselves in any danger."

CHAPTER 8

I slid the tray of chicken into the oven, then picked up the colander of blueberries. I tipped in a bunch of sugar, cornstarch, lemon peel, then added some allspice, cinnamon, and salt—all by eye. I never was one for measuring out ingredients. Following my instincts has always worked for me, and I think it allows for a bit more creativity.

Amy and Penny laid out the champagne flutes across the other countertop, and as Amy poured a little champagne into the bottom of each, Penny topped it up with orange juice and then a splash of lemonade to keep the fizz despite the small amount of wine.

"Once you're done with those," I said to Penny, "I want you to cube those potatoes and peel and slice the shallots for later. Once you've done that, can you divide this blueberry mix between the pastry cases, and we'll bake them before serving. The beans and barbecue sauce are already made, ready to be reheated later, and I'll be back in time to check on the chicken. All right?"

She looked a little taken aback, but she nodded. She wasn't used to having so much responsibility, but I had complete faith that she could do it. I had an investigation to get on with—one that I hadn't wanted to get involved in, but now that I was, I was determined to discover the truth. Walter deserved nothing less, and I couldn't deny that my mind was already whirring with questions and possibilities.

"Ready?" I asked Amy as we both picked up a tray of mimosas.

"Ready," she said.

I nodded for Penny to open the door for us, and we marched through to the coaches ahead. I placed my tray on the end table, nodding to Amy, who started handing them out. Everyone turned to look at us as we entered, and I put on my warmest smile, thinking that if I could make them feel at ease, they would be more likely to open up to me. This whole meeting and greeting thing wasn't typically part of my job, and certainly not until the food had been served and eaten. Still, I'd done enough liaising with the town council when catering events to know how to network. I was as good as the next person at getting people to open up.

I looked around at the people. So much diversity in one small space. Our passengers came from all different walks of life, and while some were engrossed by the scenery out the window, others were huddled on the couches chatting excitedly to one another. There was the odd person still looking at me or watching Amy, and they were the ones who intrigued me the most. What were they so interested in?

It struck me that whoever did this was probably wondering whether we'd discovered the body yet and how much we knew. They'd be watching us carefully for any signs of unease or panic, and they'd be wondering why nothing had happened yet. There didn't seem to be anyone in the carriage who looked anxious, though. There were smiles all round—even coming from the small, dark-haired woman who passed me by earlier. She'd clearly found a way to relax, staring out of the window and watching the world pass us by.

"Hi there," I said brightly as I approached her. She visibly jumped, and I chuckled, offering my apologies for startling her. "I'm Jessica, the chef," I said.

"Hello," she replied, although I could hear the question in her voice. She wasn't expecting anyone to speak to her, and she was wondering why I was doing so now.

"Are you enjoying the day?" I asked.

The seat next to hers was empty, but I thought it might go against me if I perched myself beside her. Instead, I remained standing, though with my back bent so we were at least eye level. I kept up with my false smile too. I felt like an air hostess.

"Er . . ." she stammered at first, shaking her head almost imperceptibly and blinking away her confusion at being spoken to. An introvert then. Not a conversationalist like some of the others I knew I would be speaking to soon enough.

"Isn't the scenery beautiful? It's like we're in the heart of nature."

"Yes," she replied eventually, clutching onto my words and running with them. "It's very peaceful."

"I'm so glad you're enjoying it, Ms. . . ."

"Dani," she said, throwing me a weak smile. "My name's Dani. Is there anything the matter?"

She seemed nervous, jumpy even, but not in a guilty way. More in a *not used to speaking to people* way. She looked worried that she would be asked to do something or that something was going to go terribly wrong.

"No, nothing the matter," I said, waving my hand in the air dismissively. "It's company policy to talk to all our passengers, check to make sure they're enjoying our services and so forth."

"Oh, I see. Well, yes," she replied, stumbling over her words. "It's perfectly pleasant, thank you."

She turned to look back out the window, but I hadn't finished. "Have you had a chance to talk to anyone else on our team?" I asked.

When she returned her gaze to me, she was clearly surprised I was still there. "No," she said simply. "To be perfectly frank, I didn't come here to talk to people. I just wanted to enjoy the ride in the peace and quiet. So, if you don't mind . . ."

She raised her eyebrows at me, and I straightened. That was my cue to leave. She had been polite enough, but she made it perfectly clear that I was bothering her. I didn't blame her; I'd be irritated by someone disturbing my afternoon with false cheeriness too.

"Of course. Amy will be around shortly with a mimosa, and we'll be dining soon. Have a lovely day, Ms . . . er . . . Dani."

She didn't reply, engrossed once again in the countryside. Well, that didn't get me very far; I discovered exactly zilch and I was in exactly the same position as I was ten minutes ago. I sighed as I looked around at the rest of the passengers. This was going to be more difficult than any of us anticipated.

"There you are, Jessica, dear."

I felt a hand brush near my arm, and I turned to see Dorothy beaming up at me. She had such a capacity for happiness and joviality, and it always made me smile to see the way in which she responded to these trips. I hoped to be like Dorothy one day, enjoying life for the sake of it and taking what comes with a brightness that can only come with letting go of your daily stresses.

"Hey, Dorothy. How are you enjoying the trip?"

"Oh, it's just lovely dear," she said. "I just spotted a Blackpoll Warbler! It's a little early to see them, but I did!" She paused. "What are you doing out of the kitchen? Is everything all right?"

So, it was noticeable then that there was a difference in what we were doing. I tried not to show my surprise at her question, laughing it off instead.

"You know, I love my job, Dorothy, but I must admit being locked away in the kitchen all the time and missing the fun out here can get a bit boring. Penny's doing so well in her training, I thought I'd get her a bit more responsibility today. It's about time."

"There's something fishy going on if you ask me."

I spun around to face Carter, who had still not moved from his position. Both regulars, they often sat opposite one another. They had a habit of bickering, but I got the impression it was welcome. They each enjoyed it as much as the other, almost like it was a feature of the excursions.

"No, we're not having fish. We're having chicken," I said in a vain attempt at lighting the mood. It didn't work. Carter narrowed his eyes at me.

"You know full well what I mean, Ms. Preston," he said, the use of my surname a clear indication of his feelings. I glanced down at the empty pages of his notebook. I guessed it was a tough day for him; it seemed like he hadn't written a thing since he got on the train. "There are far too many secrets on this train, and I'm determined to find out what they are!"

"I have no idea what you're talking about, Carter," I said softly. "I can assure you that there are no secrets or mysteries or surprises. Everything is completely normal."

If only, I thought bitterly. At the very least, I was reasonably certain there would be no *further* surprises. Especially not if we worked out who did the deed sooner rather than later.

"I don't believe you," Carter said. He crossed his arms over his chest, somehow making himself look like a moody teenager—quite impressive, given his forty-something years.

I shrugged. "Well, there's not a lot I can do about that, I'm afraid, other than reiterate, once more, that everything is perfectly fine. Are you not enjoying the day, Carter?"

"Oh, of course he is," Dorothy said with a wave of her hand behind me. "He enjoys being a miserable old so-and-so. Don't listen to him, Jessica, dear. I don't get why the old goat doesn't write a mystery instead of this literary nonsense he's going for. You should write what people want to read, Carter dear, and mysteries are big business these days, you know. The sooner you accept that you're no Hemmingway, the better."

"Oh, go back to your bird watching," he snapped in a fluster, and I had to force my lips together to stop myself from laughing. "Even Hemingway had to start somewhere, and I am so much better than a *mystery*! As for you, Ms. Preston, while I am enjoying the day, as I always do on this train, I must insist on knowing what is going on. It is plainly obvious to me that something untoward has happened, and that's why the train stopped back near Golden. Why don't you just admit there is something going on?"

I offered him a humoring smile, all the while biting the inside of my cheek to stop myself from snapping at him. "I'm sorry, Carter, but I really don't know what you're talking about. Enjoy your mimosa, won't you?"

I turned and left before he could say anything else. I knew he would not let it drop. He would wear me down until I gave in and admitted what had happened. One of things about being a good detective—or being good at anything, I figured—was knowing when to walk away. It did get me wondering, though. As far as I was concerned, we'd done a good job at keeping everything under wraps. Carter being suspicious was peculiar, and it got my attention.

Don't be silly, Jessica! I shook that thought out of my head as soon as it arrived there. Carter was *always* suspicious. It didn't matter the journey or what had happened on it, Carter would have something to complain about or question. It was just who he was, and I half thought the complaints were part of the experience for him—spotting what we did or didn't do wrong was all part of the appeal.

Making my way down the aisle, I spotted the woman I knew would want to talk to me: the winemaker from Napa, Beverly Lyonel. I took in a deep breath then marched up to her.

"Hello, Mrs. Lyonel. How are you enjoying the trip?"

"This is such a beautiful area," she said breathlessly, not taking her eyes from the window. "It's incredible. The fires were entirely devastating, but looking at this place . . . I wonder if it was a blessing in disguise. To move to the gold country . . ."

"It is wonderful," I said, feeling equally wistful. "I'm so lucky to live in such a place, and to get to travel through it day-in, day-out. You said you had some questions for me?"

That snapped her out of her daze. She turned to face me, all business again. "Yes, yes, I do. As I said earlier, I'm hoping to restart here. Open a new winery and start production going again. I'd like to open it to the public for tours and whatnot too. I know my product very well, and I know it's a good one. What I'm not sure about is how well received it will be here."

"You would have no concerns in that respect, Mrs. Lyonel," I reassured her. "The wine industry in Northern California is booming at the moment, or so I'm led to believe. The climate is just right, and the earth is ripe for planting. I believe you could make a good winery here."

"Yes, I know," she said plainly, looking at me like I was stupid. "I understand perfectly well what is required to produce good quality wine. That's not what I'm asking."

I laughed nervously. "In that case, I'm not sure what I can offer you," I said with a shrug. "I don't know a lot about the industry, other than from a consumption point of view, of course." I tried to laugh again, but I could see from her expression that she was not amused. Did nothing please this woman?

"I want to know about *trends*. I want facts and figures, not opinions. Graphs, even." She didn't want much then. I pressed my lips together, listening to her list her requirements and wondering how on earth she thought she was going to get any of that from the chef of a luxury train. "I mean, what about tourism?"

"What about it?" I asked and she huffed.

"Is there a lot of it around here?"

"It's increasing by the day," I said.

"What percentage, roughly, of your passengers would you say are tourists to locals?"

"I . . . er . . . I'm not quite sure, to be honest, Mrs. Lyonel. You might be better off talking to the manager, Greg Kendrick, about that sort of thing. I'm more of a creative person than a numbers person."

She sighed, shaking her head sadly. "That much I can see. I did try talking to that Walter Mansell fellow. What is he again? IT specialist?"

"Yes, that's right," I said, shocked she even knew him, let alone had spoken to him. Walter kept himself to himself and rarely conversed with the passengers.

"I would have thought with a job like that, he'd have been more in the know when it comes to numbers and trends, but he was entirely useless. Really, anyone would think I was trying to get blood from him, the way he reacted to my questioning."

I could well imagine it too. Walter never did well with forceful people, or even women in general, and Beverly Lyonel was nothing if not forceful.

"Walter is . . ." *Was.* "He's not so good when it comes to situations he perceives as conflict."

Beverly visibly paled, looking back at me with horror. Or was it fear? "Conflict! To suggest my asking questions was anything of the sort is . . . well, it's simply not true."

"I'm sure he would understand if you wished to discuss the matter with him," I said, hoping to rule her out if she suggested going to look for him.

I hadn't really thought through what I would do if she leapt up and

61

insisted on searching for him. I couldn't very well let her roam around the train again.

Who knows what she will find?

She pursed her lips and turned away. "No, I don't think so," she said, staring out of the window once again. "If he does not wish to talk with me, then I do not wish to talk with him."

Luckily—or perhaps unluckily, depending on how you looked at it —I didn't need to worry. Had it been pride that stopped her from pursuing the matter, or hurt that he would think in such a way /

Or could it be that she already knows how pointless it will be, because she knows he was dead?

CHAPTER 9

$\mathscr{A}$t that moment, Greg appeared, having finished talking to those in the first coach. He looked seriously at me and I went to talk to him, our voices nothing more than quiet whispers.

"Hey," I said "How'd it go?"

Greg shook his head. "I am so far out of my depth," he admitted. "I have no idea what I'm looking for."

"Anyone say anything out of the ordinary? Or seem like they were trying to hide anything?"

"Yes and no. I'm not sure whether I'm just reading too much into their reactions, given what I know."

"Yeah, I know what you mean. Every little thing seems to stand out."

"Exactly. What about her?" He nudged his chin in Beverly Lyonel's direction and I frowned at him.

"I don't think she's involved. I don't know why, just a feeling I get." I paused as we both watched Mrs. Lyonel staring out of the window, clearly deep in thought. Her brow was furrowed, like something was bothering her. "Although she did say she knew Walter."

"Really?" He turned to look at me, wide-eyed. "Apparently, Ralph overheard Walter arguing with—and these are his words, not mine —'some rich lady going on about wineries and computer trends.'"

"Certainly sounds like her," I agreed. "But why would they be arguing?"

"Perhaps arguing was the wrong word. But from what I hear, she was haranguing him, demanding more and more information from him. And you know what Walter's like . . . *was* like. Wouldn't say boo to a goose."

I looked back over to Mrs. Lyonel, still lost in her own world. She was persuasive and determined, that's certain, and she didn't seem like the type to take no for an answer.

But that didn't mean she was capable of murder.

Did it?

"Anyway, Jessie." Greg put a hand onto my elbow, making me jump and gasp, swinging back round to him.

I was so surprised I didn't even correct my name. All I could think about was that hand, the feeling of it burning through me.

"Yes?" I said quickly.

"I just wanted to say thank you, again. For doing this with me. I don't know what I would have done without you."

He smiled warmly at me and I squirmed, shifting away from his hand. I didn't know what had got into him. He had gone from being temperamental and moody to gazing longingly at me like a teenage boy. He couldn't possibly want us to reunite, could he? I groaned as silently as I could, praying Vanessa wasn't right.

"Excuse me." Dani barged past, pushing through us to get to the door.

Greg and I automatically separated, letting her past, but I couldn't help wondering what she could possibly want at that end of the train. Then it came to me—the facilities. I shook my head. Greg was right; everything seemed suspicious when you were searching for something.

Before she went through the door, she looked over her shoulder at Greg, catching his eye for a beat too long. Greg looked back at her with a frown, confusion written across his face.

"What is it?" I asked.

"I'm not sure," he said, still watching as the door swung closed. "I

64

think . . . I think I recognize her from somewhere, I just can't put my finger on where."

I snorted, unable to stop myself. "From the way she looked at you, she knew you too. A one-night stand you've forgotten about, maybe?" He looked obviously hurt by my jibe, and I instantly regretted it.

"I'm not as bad as you think, you know, Jessica."

"No, you're right. I know. Sorry."

"Anyway, how's the food prep coming along?" he asked.

"Fine. I'm going to jump off at . . ." I looked out the window and realized where we were. We'd passed the little station with the market without stopping. I stared openmouthed for a moment, then turned on Greg. "Hey! Why didn't we stop?"

"I thought it was best not to," Greg said. "I thought you'd be pleased. It'll get us into the main station earlier."

"And you didn't think to discuss this with anyone else?" I asked, horrified he could think to do such a thing.

"It's like you said earlier, Jessica. I *am* the manager. I am under no obligation to discuss my decisions with anyone else."

"In that case, as chef, I'd best get back to the kitchen," I said, giving him my frostiest glare.

"Good idea. I'll come with you. It's about time we reconvened."

I didn't look at him, nor at anyone else, as I marched back to my kitchen, or murder HQ as I felt like calling it now. I couldn't believe Greg arranged it so the train didn't stop and hadn't told me!

So much for salmon and brie!

"OH, HEY. YOU'RE BACK," VANESSA SAID AS WE WALKED IN. HOW SHE'D managed to pass us, I had no idea, but she and Amy were already in the kitchen, and Vanessa seemed eager to share.

"What did you learn?" I asked.

"That motorcars are inordinately hot, that engineers are a grumpy lot, and that dead bodies are not as scary as I thought they were."

"You looked at the body?" I asked, aghast at the idea.

She shrugged. "Just a sneak peek. I lifted the corner of the blanket, that's all."

"But why?" I asked. "You can be so morbid sometimes, Ness!"

"I had to check for clues, didn't I?" she said. "And, admittedly, I was a little bit curious."

"Ugh." I shook my head and looked around to see if everyone else felt the same.

From Penny's open mouth and Amy's shocked expression, I'd say they did. Only Greg was smiling. In fact, he seemed incredibly relaxed and calm—quite a stark difference from the fear and stress that were in his eyes earlier.

Could he have got over the shock so easily?

I didn't want to think badly of Greg, no matter how crazy he drove me, but seeing him like this reminded me that the murderer really could be anyone, and that I had to keep an eye on everything.

Including Greg.

"You didn't mess up the crime scene, did you?" I asked. "The authorities will want to look at that."

"Of course not," Vanessa said.

"Or accidentally leave one of your own hairs," Penny said with a snort. "Imagine being blamed for the murder because of that!"

Vanessa paled but didn't reply.

"Did you find any clues then?" I asked.

"Any stray hairs?" Greg asked.

"No hairs," she admitted. "Other than the ones on his head. I did see a footprint in the dirt though. Looked like a man's to me, but I've got to admit, the entirety of my forensic knowledge comes from TV, so perhaps I'm not the best one to judge."

"No worse than the rest of us, Ness," I said.

"I don't think it means anything," Greg said, perhaps a little too quickly. "Footprint like that, it could be anyone's. All the worker's go through there. I'm surprised there's not more of them."

Vanessa looked down at Greg's feet and laughed. "About your size, I reckon, Greg," she said, teasing him, but the knot in my chest tightened as I watched him scowl at her in return.

Could it be?

"So we've got a footprint in a heavy traffic area. Anything else? Maybe something more specific?"

"Actually, yes," Vanessa said, grinning proudly. "One of them engineer fellas said he saw that Beverly woman—you know, the one who accosted us on our way in. She was coming out of the motorcar, apparently."

"What on earth was she doing in there?" Amy asked. "That's strictly staff only. Even I don't go in there, and I'm allowed."

"Arguing with Walter," Greg said. "Ralph overheard them."

"Now that you mention it, I saw Mrs. Lyonel hanging around by your office earlier, Greg," I said. "No idea what she was doing there."

"Maybe she was just using the facilities," Vanessa pointed out. "But there's definitely something odd about her. We need to find out more."

"One to keep an eye on for sure," Greg said. "Prime suspect, I'd say."

I narrowed my eyes at him. That was the second time he'd been quick to blame Mrs. Lyonel.

How could he be so certain?

"How about you, Amy? Did you overhear anything or see something of interest?"

"No," Amy said simply. "They all look guilty to me."

"It can't be *all* of them, though," Vanessa said. "That's just your imagination running wild."

"Maybe," Amy agreed. "But everyone's guilty of something, aren't they? Perhaps I'm not so good at pinpointing which is murder and which isn't."

"How about you, Penny?"

Her head shot up in my direction, clearly surprised to have been singled out as she diligently poured blueberries into tart cases.

"What about me?" she asked.

"Have you heard anything? Seen anything?"

"How could I have?" she asked. "I've been in here, doing all the things you asked of me."

She sounded panicked, nervous even. She was right, she hadn't left the kitchen, but as we were talking, she stayed a bit too quiet. Quiet was not something Penny managed often, usually letting her mouth run away with her before her mind kicked into action. She was a typical teenager, and keeping quiet in a situation like this was not typical. I got the sense that she was listening intently, trying to gather as much information as she could.

Either that, or she was not speaking in the hopes we'd forget she was there and we'd slip up, say something we didn't mean to say in front of her.

But why? To pass on to someone, maybe?

For goodness' sake, Jessica!

"You're right," I said. "I'm being silly. And you've done a wonderful job. We'll get those tarts in the oven as soon as the chicken comes out. Speaking of which . . ."

I pulled the oven gloves down from the hook, slipped them on, and pulled the tray of bacon-wrapped chicken breasts from the oven. I transferred them to a cooling rack to rest, then turned to the stove, thinking to make a start on the soup.

My hat. I needed my hat. I snatched it up from the side and pulled it down over my head.

I was foolish to think anything even remotely bad about Penny. We'd worked together for the entire two months since I'd taken on the train kitchen. I really did have nothing to worry about. Her quietness was more likely down to the fact that she genuinely had nothing to add, or maybe the morbidity of the subject was putting her off. She was awfully young to be dealing with death at all, and a murder was even worse.

I couldn't keep thinking badly of every single person on board.

"What's next?" Vanessa asked.

"We need to get the burgers on the griddle. The sauce and the beans need reheating, and the taters need cooking. Then we need to get the tarts in—"

"I meant with the investigation," Vanessa said dryly, looking up at me from beneath her lashes.

"Oh, yeah," I said. "That." I lit the stove and put the pan on, drizzling a touch of oil into it. "That's going to have to go on pause for a while. We've got a lot of hungry guests out there."

"I'll get back out there," Greg said. "Liaise some more. You never know when someone might slip up. Think I might focus my attentions on that Beverly Lyonel."

"Don't," I said over my shoulder. "Spread your time out amongst all the guests. It'll look odd if you don't, and I don't believe we've got enough evidence to convict Mrs. Lyonel of the crime just yet."

"Whatever you say," Greg said, mock saluting me. *Idiot.*

"Amy, go check everything is good to go in the dining room."

"What about me?" Vanessa said. She'd come up behind me and was standing on her tiptoes, peering over my shoulder at what I was doing. She was hungry, I could tell. It was like she gave off a vibe when she was hungry. "Correct me if I'm wrong, but I seem to remember a certain chef promising me a burger or two."

I raised my eyebrow at her over my shoulder. "You'll get your burgers, don't worry. But all in good time."

It was then the knock came at the door. We were all so tense that the simple noise made us all jump, then fall back laughing at our own silliness. Even so, for someone to knock, there must be something wrong. It could only be a passenger; all the staff know they can just walk in.

With a frown and a quick shared glance with Vanessa, I opened the door. There was a young man there, about eighteen years old, wearing jeans and a white button-down shirt with a clipboard hugged to his chest. His face was pocked with acne scars, and he looked absolutely terrified at the prospect of speaking to anyone.

"You must be Lucas," I said, guessing him to be the intern straight away.

"Y-yes, Ms. Preston."

"Jessica's fine," I said. "And you don't need to knock. There's nothing secret going on in here."

"Okay." He looked down at the clipboard, then around the room. When he spotted Penny, his awkward smile grew into a broad grin, and he waggled his fingers at her in a wave. "Hi, Penny."

"Hi, Lucas," she replied, equally coyly. Looking at them both, I wondered how on earth they began speaking to each other in the first place. Neither was particularly forthcoming.

"Aw, like little lovebirds," Vanessa said.

I widened my eyes at her, begging her not to embarrass them. It may have been a long time ago, but we both remembered what it was like to be teenagers and in the first flushes of love.

"What can we do for you, Lucas?" I asked, clapping my hands loudly to bring the attention back to the moment.

"I came to remind you that it's fifteen minutes until service," he said.

"Thank you, Lucas. That's very professional of you." I spun back around to the group. "Greg, get out and do what you need to do. As for the rest of you, it's all hands-on deck! We don't have much time left."

"But—"

"But nothing, Vanessa," I said, cocking my head and winking at her. "You persuaded me to get involved in this murder investigation, so I'm blaming you for the holdup. Besides, you gotta earn that burger somehow."

CHAPTER 10

"*W*ell done, team," I said as the last of the plates left the kitchen and we fell into the lull that always happens between service and clean up.

"I've got to say, Jessica, I didn't realize quite what this job entails," Vanessa said. "I'm surprised you're not exhausted every night when you get home."

"I often am," I said with a chuckle. "But I think we can all agree that today has not been your average day. For starters, I'm normally much more organized than this. I usually have a plan before I even get on board."

"And there's not normally a dead body in the motorcar," Amy added.

Vanessa put a hand to her chest and gasped in mock surprise. "You're telling me there's not a murder investigation every day?"

"No, no," I said, looking at the ceiling, pretending to remember. "I can honestly say this is a first."

"And hopefully the last," Amy said.

"And we haven't even solved this one yet." I frowned at the floor, leaning back against the countertop. I had not forgotten about the investigation, nor poor Walter, of course, but I had been able to focus on kitchen duties for a bit. Now my mind began racing again. I felt like I suspected everyone and no one at the same time.

How do real life detectives manage it?

"It's been a fantastic service, though," Penny said, pulling my attention back to the kitchen.

Her smile beamed across the coach, and I could see that she was thrumming with energy. Some people couldn't handle the stress and the pressure of a kitchen, like my own daughter, Frannie. I'd wanted so much for her to enjoy cooking and baking alongside me, but she'd fallen in love with gold, just like her father. Together they ran *The Nugget*, the premiere gold shop in all Northern California.

But not Penny. Penny was definitely a chef in the making. She'd caught the buzz, and she wasn't likely to quit any time soon.

"You've done really well today, Penny," I said, smiling at her. "Perhaps next week we can get you started on an appetizer of your own, something of your choice—though with my approval, of course. If it's a hit, we can add it to the menu permanently."

"Really?" She looked at me with such excitement. "That would be epic! And all it took was Walter dying."

"No," I replied firmly, looking at her in all seriousness. "Walter dying is tragic and, admittedly, has taken me away from the kitchen today. But you're getting this opportunity because you earned it and no other reason. Understand?"

Penny nodded frantically.

"Good girl. Now, all of you grab yourselves something to eat. We've got about forty minutes, maybe an hour, before we're back to full action."

"Does that mean . . ." Vanessa looked at me hopefully.

"Yes," I laughed. "It's burger time. In fact, I already prepared it."

"Thank goodness!" she gushed. "I'll fade away if I don't eat soon."

"Right. Out, all of you," I said, ushering them with my arms. "Go into the dining room and give me a bit of time to think."

They shuffled out together, chattering amongst themselves like a bunch of kids, even Vanessa. I watched them go with a smile, then sighed and fell back onto the stool, burying my face in my hands. I was at a loss as to where to go now in terms of the investigation. Yes, I was captivated; I'd been hooked by the mystery and dearly wanted to work it out. But I was starting to doubt my capabilities. I was no detective, and I never would be. Greg was right when he said I enjoyed a puzzle, but this was completely different, and I was worried I was doing Walter a disservice.

I looked out the window. We were going over a trestle bridge, the wind picking up in the open air and buffeting the train. The water below us shimmered in the light, the surface rippling in the breeze. It was amazing how one tiny disturbance could affect the water all the way at the other side of the river, the rippling continuing potentially for miles.

Life was a bit like that. Something could happen, and the effects of it could ripple through the rest of your time on earth. What happened today could cause you to behave in a certain way tomorrow, be it for better or worse. Like murder.

I got to my feet with a gasp, my eyes darting across the floor as the thought ran through me. That was it. Something had happened in Walter's life that had caused a ripple effect. And now, too, there would be ripples caused by his death. I had to get out there and look for the ripples.

When I entered the restaurant coach, the atmosphere was jubilant and full of laughter. Cutlery clanked against plates and glasses clinked together as they celebrated the success of their trip. I put my hands behind my back and leant against the doorframe, watching carefully. I was glad to see everyone happy—and calm, for that matter. We made the right decision in continuing with the day. I could only imagine what a mess we'd be in now if we'd stopped the train and told everyone the truth. As it was, we could investigate without causing chaos.

On the small table to my right, Vanessa tucked hungrily into her second burger—she had an impressive appetite, even in the direst of circumstances—while Amy and Penny pushed their food around their plates.

Then there was Greg. He moved seamlessly around the coach, sipping slowly at a suspiciously full mimosa. I suspected that was *not* his first one, but I wouldn't argue about it now. Everyone seemed happy enough, and it didn't feel like there was a shortage. He wore a huge smile, and the creases of his brow had all but disappeared as he went from table to table, charming each of the passengers in turn.

He was like a different man from the one we'd seen earlier. He was calm, collected, ready to face anything.

Could that simply be a consequence of having us all on his side?

Or was there something else that gave him the easy air and the idea he could relax?

More likely, I decided, it was evidence of how good he was at his job—not only because he kept profits up, but because he was good with the customers too.

He looked up at me and threw me a warm smile, the twinkle in his eye making me chuckle and look away. I had no desire to get back with him, obviously—that ship had long ago sailed—but I had to admit he was not as bad as I thought. Maybe the tumultuous relationship we'd had over the last two months of working together was necessary in order to get us to where we were today. I'd read him wrong; I had fought back when it wasn't required. We would make a good team going forward, that much was clear.

I wandered through the tables, greeting passengers and receiving feedback. The food, despite the mad panic earlier, had been a resounding success.

"Compliments to the chef," Mrs. Wallis said, raising her champagne flute in my direction.

"Thank you," I replied with a small bow.

They would be back, and if not, they'd tell their friends about what a wonderful time they'd had. That made it all worth it.

"Jessica, dear, I must say, you've outdone yourself today."

"That's very kind of you to say, Dorothy."

"I was a little skeptical when Walter told me about the change in plans—you know how much I hate change. But actually, what you prepared was a great compromise, a gourmet barbecue like no other."

"I'm so glad you enjoyed it, Dorothy," I replied.

Even Carter complimented the meal, albeit reluctantly, and that was a big deal for him. He must have truly enjoyed it.

The door between the two restaurant cars had been wedged open for service, and I could see through to the far end. Dani was there, sat facing me, but her expression was dark, and her arms were crossed over her chest. Her eyes followed Greg, an almost ominous glint to them, and she hadn't even touched the food in front of her. She was an odd one, for sure, but it amused me to see the scorn she directed at Greg.

Definitely an ex-lover.

One Greg had wronged at some point, even if he couldn't quite remember it. She was his type, after all—slim, with dark hair and tan skin. I wondered if he'd picked up a stalker and found myself chuckling at the idea. He wouldn't like that at all, but it would be fair punishment if he had led the poor woman on.

"Jessica, a word, if I may."

I inwardly groaned at the sound of Mrs. Lyonel's voice. I should have known she would have a problem about something—and that she would find a way to complain about it. Greg met my gaze again, and he nodded in her direction. He obviously still thought she had a hand in all this. I shook my head at him, but he nodded again, urging me to find out more.

"Mrs. Lyonel, is everything all right?" I asked, pasting on a smile.

Wherever you worked and whatever you did, there was always one customer like Mrs. Lyonel, a busybody who meant well but was exhausting all the same. I always thought Carter was our one, but he was a breeze compared to her.

That was one of the main reasons I didn't truly consider her a suspect. People like her exist in all walks of life, and she didn't mean any harm. She knew what she wanted, and she would find a way to get it. If that made her capable of murder, then there were a lot of other people in the world capable of it too.

"No, actually," she said. "I was not at all happy with the meal. I was given the impression that you were highly trained and understood what *gourmet* meant. But you served us fancy barbecue food instead. That is not what I signed up for."

"I'm sorry to hear you were disappointed," I said, and genuinely, too. I didn't like the idea of anyone being dissatisfied with what I served. "It can be difficult to keep everyone happy, and I know several people on this train were expecting barbecue food."

"That's no excuse," she said firmly. "You shouldn't advertise it as one thing if you're going to serve it as another. I really must insist on some compensation."

"You are quite right, Mrs. Lyonel."

"I am?"

She looked surprised that I had agreed with her, that she had won so easily. I could see Greg watching us from behind her, shaking his head firmly. I smiled and raised my brows at him, then turned back to Mrs. Lyonel.

"Of course you're right. You should have received what you were led to believe you would receive. Why don't you talk to our manager, Greg?"

I pointed in his direction, and she turned to look. His expression of abject horror quickly turned into a customer service smile. He picked up a mimosa from the table and walked over to us, holding the glass out to her. She took it, though she looked down at it disapprovingly.

"Don't think you can buy me off with a glass of fizzy juice," she snapped. "Even that's not the promised champagne!"

"No," he replied, his eyes sparkling at her over the top of his own glass. He took a sip, then smacked his lips together in satisfaction. "It's much, much better," he said. "You should try it."

She thrust the glass back at him and he took hold of it, placing his own down on the table to his left.

"I don't think so," she replied firmly.

"Your loss," he said, taking a sip from the second glass.

"I expect to be fully compensated," she demanded.

"Naturally, Mrs. Lyonel."

I wondered what on earth he was doing. He was riling her rather than calming her, and that was not at all how it was supposed to go. But what he said next made it all come clear, and I marveled once again at how good he was at his job—and how well he had hidden that fact until now.

He took another sip, opening and closing his mouth rapidly and looking at the ceiling, as though taste-testing the drink.

"You know, Mrs. Lyonel, I think you might be right. This is subpar. I've been considering for a while getting a new wine supplier. I don't suppose you know anyone who may be able to help with that, do you?"

The smile returned to her face in an instant, and she looked almost flustered by the potential business. "Why, yes, I do," she said. "I myself will be opening a winery in Golden in the very near future. I'm sure we could come to some sort of arrangement. My range of wines has won awards, you know."

"I would expect nothing less from a woman of your so very obvious capabilities," he said.

He looked over her head at me and winked, but I simply shook my head and turned away, just as he was taking another sip of Mrs. Lyonel's mimosa. I'd leave them to work out the details while I continued with our investigation. And there was the kitchen to clean —the absolute worst part of my job.

I jumped when the door between the two restaurant coaches slammed shut, and I spun back around to see what had happened. It had been wedged open; somebody would have had to physically close it. A porter, perhaps? Or one of the engineers? I frowned at the door, trying to figure it out, when I heard a glass fall to the floor.

I looked just in time to see Greg's mimosa splash up from the smashed glass, splattering Mrs. Lyonel's legs. I was about to reprimand him when he himself fell backwards, landing heavily against a table and causing all the crockery to smash around him. His face had turned the color of beetroot, and he clutched at his throat, but before he fell unconscious, he managed to utter a single word.

"Help!"

CHAPTER 11

"What the . . ." I heard Vanessa's voice behind me, and I could picture her slowly rising out of her seat, her face drained of color and her eyes bulging as if she wanted to see but didn't want to see all at the same time.

Me? I froze to the spot for what felt like forever, but in truth was no more than a few seconds. Everything slowed, and I watched the glass shatter and stared in horror as Greg fell to the floor, a look of sheer terror on his face.

Passengers leapt out of his way, backing up as though whatever had happened to Greg might be catching. I could see they were screaming, and that things were crashing to the floor, but I could hear nothing but the blood rushing through my own ears. As he fell, he clutched his throat as though he couldn't breathe, and on his way down, he desperately grasped for something to steady himself, finding only the tablecloth and bringing a rain of broken crockery down on top of him.

He fell, and his head bounced off the floor before coming to a rest. That's when I kicked into action, the noise and the shouts of the carriage rushing back to me.

"Everybody get back!" I called.

I hurried through the now standing bodies until I reached Greg, and I threw my arms wide to stop anyone else approaching. We needed space. *Greg* needed space.

"Somebody get a doctor!" Mrs. Lyonel screamed.

"And how in the hell are we going to do that when we're halfway up a mountain?" someone shouted back.

"Can anyone do first aid?"

"Stay back," I repeated, diving onto the floor next to him. "Give us space!"

I was the resident first-aider and I had experience in this sort of thing. As much as I hated being involved, I knew it was up to me to help—and to try and keep everyone calm. Besides, it was Greg! I had to do something.

"Greg," I said quickly. "Greg?"

No response. I put my hand to his forehead—it was oddly cold to the touch. My fingers felt around his neck for a pulse. It was there, but weak, and his breaths came ragged and uneven. I yanked at his shirt, pulling open the top two buttons to give him more space to breathe. With a grunt of effort, I managed to get him into the recovery position, one hand resting under his head, his right knee over his left leg.

My eyes searched his face, his body, for any sort of clues as to what had happened.

Heart attack?

No, he would have clutched his chest or his arm, not his throat. Stroke, then? Again, couldn't be—he had none of the typical symptoms. Then what?

It came to me with a gasp, and I couldn't believe I hadn't thought of it sooner, given what had already happened that day. There was a murderer on board, for goodness sake! And Greg was intent on finding them.

"What is it, Jessica?" Vanessa asked. "What's happened?" She was on her knees beside me now, though I hadn't noticed her arrival, and I could feel the fearful energy coming off her in waves.

"I think someone slipped something into his drink," I said, leaning over him to make sure, yet again, that his airways were clear.

"Poison!"

I glanced at her and nodded wordlessly. I hadn't wanted to say *poison*, but I think she was right. She nodded back at me, understanding me perfectly—this was the work of our murderer. It had to be.

"What are we going to do?" she asked, quieter this time, pointedly ignoring those around us.

"I . . ."

"You know," Carter said. "I read somewhere that—"

"Shut up, Carter," Vanessa snapped, looking over her shoulder at him. "And back off. Jessica knows what she's doing."

While I appreciated the vote of confidence, I wasn't sure I felt the same about the pressure. A man's life hung in the balance—for the second time that day—and my mind was blank. Just as I was no police investigator, I was no paramedic either.

But there has to be something!

"What makes you think he's been poisoned?" Vanessa asked. I knew what she was doing—asking me simple questions to get my brain working and keep my panic away. Good old Vanessa, she always knew what I needed. I nodded, then explained my reasoning.

"Look at the way his eyes are bulging," I said. "And that sickly tinge to his flesh. I don't know what poison it could be, but it looks pretty fast acting."

"So, what do we do? What's the next step?" she asked, looking intently at me, silently willing me to fix this.

I sat back on my heels and looked down at him, my eyes darting over him as I tried to think through all the training I'd had over the years. What to do, how to act. My mind was crowded with screams and words and images.

"Should we make him sick?" Amy asked, leaning down. Her words were rapid and filled with panic, her eyes shining with fear.

"No, definitely not that," I said. "Sometimes that can do more harm than good. Amy, go fetch a blanket."

"Should we move him?" Dorothy asked.

"Yes, but not yet," I replied, putting my fingertips to my temples and closing my eyes. "Let me think."

Again, the moment felt like a lifetime, the tension high and taut, all eyes on me and Greg. I had to do something!

"I've got it!" I jumped to my feet and ran—or tried to run—to the kitchen. I had to push my way through the gawking audience, no one wanting to move in case they missed some of the excitement. "Get out of my way!" I roared.

I skidded across the kitchen floor, only just catching myself on the countertop before I fell.

Slow down, Jessica. We don't need more casualties!

I snatched the green satchel from the top shelf in the far corner, pulling it down and spilling its contents at the same time.

Quickly! I rummaged through, searching for what I was looking for, discarding bandages and safety pins and alcohol wipes and burn cream, my fingers shaking as I searched.

"Got it!"

By the time I got back to Greg, the crowd's terrified screams and shouts of fear had lessened to worried murmurs. Most had fallen back into their seats and now talked in hushed, hurried whispers, occasionally twisting their head to check nothing else had happened. There were only a few stragglers still standing.

I popped the lid of the pill bottle, tipped one into my hand, then put it to Greg's lips. Of course, he was unresponsive. I took a deep breath, praying I was doing the right thing, but when I glanced at Vanessa, she nodded her encouragement at me. I forced the pill into his mouth and held his jaw closed. His body did what it was designed to do, and he swallowed automatically.

I sat back with a sigh of relief, hoping I had got to him in time.

"What's that?" Vanessa asked.

"Activated charcoal. It stops the body from absorbing toxins and drugs, but it'll only work if we've managed to get to him before the poison hits his bloodstream."

"And that'll work?" Carter asked.

I answered without taking my eyes off Greg, watching his face carefully for some sort of response. "I think so," I said. "I've never had to use it before, but that's what it's supposed to do, yeah."

Vanessa sat back on her haunches, and I could feel her looking at me, her eyes wide with astonishment. Greg's skin was returning to a normal shade and his breathing seemed more regular. I nodded again, thinking that had to be a good sign. Right?

"How on earth do you know such things, Jessica?" Vanessa asked. "And why do you have it at hand? The longer I know you, the more you surprise me."

I shrugged. "I guess it's just an important thing to have around a kitchen. You know, where people are ingesting things. You never know what will happen."

"Your food's not *that* bad," Vanessa said with a snort.

I shot her a glare, though secretly I was glad for her dark humor, especially now that I could see Greg beginning to squirm. I started to answer, but before I could, Greg groaned.

"You're all right, Greg," I said, leaning back over him. I'm not sure I ever really believed in activated charcoal, but seeing it work its magic made me thankful I'd brought it on board.

He opened his eyes. They shone dully and he looked about him, dazed, and I wasn't certain he knew where he was for a moment.

"Jessie," he croaked. "What . . . what happened?"

"We don't know exactly yet," I said. "But we need to get you to the infirmary as soon as possible."

That's when I heard Lucas's voice, demanding to know what was going on in the most undemanding and unauthoritative tone possible —a feat only a nervous intern can achieve.

"Let him through," I said, looking up at those who blocked the way.

When Lucas finally set eyes on Greg, the pink of his cheeks turned white and he took a staggering step backwards, his eyes as wide as Greg's were.

"Lucas?" I asked, worried that something had happened to him. But no, he was scared, nothing more. I wondered how he'd cope if and when he became manager himself and had to deal with situations like this.

"What's going on?" he managed to ask, though he still didn't come any closer.

"We need to get him to the infirmary," I said, eyeing Lucas carefully. "He's all right, we caught it in time, but he needs rest, and as soon as we stop, he needs proper medical attention. Understood?"

He stared at Greg for a moment longer, mouth hanging open. Greg had closed his eyes again, his arm across his stomach, but his breathing was slow and steady. He looked more like he was sleeping than had just been drugged, and I took that to be a good sign.

"Lucas?"

His eyes finally flickered to me, and he nodded. "Oh, yeah, yeah," he said, before bending down to take one of Greg's arms, assisting me in helping him up.

"Here, Jessica," Carter said, throwing me a sympathetic look I'd never have thought possible from him before. "Let me. Looks like you've got enough to deal with here." He took Greg's arm from me, and the three of them made their way haltingly down the train.

I closed my eyes, a hand held across my face, and I sighed. It had certainly been an eventful day so far, and it was nowhere near over. I looked out of the window to gauge where we were. Whoever had shouted was right—we were weaving through the mountains. It was obvious there was no cell service and definitely no mobile data. What it also meant was that we were a good hour away from stopping anywhere, or therefore getting help.

I shook my head. I'd murder Greg myself if I wasn't so morally bound to this idea of not taking life. He'd got me caught up in this whole thing. At least I knew one thing now though. Those dark thoughts that told me Greg could have killed Walter were wrong. He was a victim, too, and almost another corpse.

Turning back to the group of panicked passengers, I clapped my hands together and smiled broadly. "Now that we've got rid of him, the real party can start," I quipped in a poor attempt to lighten the mood.

While Vanessa laughed—good old Vanessa—everyone else looked either horrified or confused. Why was it she could make a joke in the middle of the most horrendous situations, but when I tried it, I fell flat on my face? Guess I should just stick to baking . . . and solving murders, for today at least.

"All right," I said, dropping the smile and looking at them with sincerity. These poor people were scared, and I'd tried to make a joke!

What an idiot!

"Listen, we are doing the very best we can, and I can assure you that we will find who did this. There is no need to worry. We've got everything under control."

I had their rapt attention now, and I turned slowly, taking in every face. They were all there. Even those from the second carriage had crowded in, filling the doorway and spilling through into this one. I wanted to see their reactions, the looks on their faces. *Someone* had to give something away, didn't they?

The only one who wasn't looking at me was Beverly Lyonel, who had returned to her seat and was staring pointedly out of the window. Her mouth was set in a firm line, and there was a hardness about her eyes.

Was it fear? Or did she have something to hide?

"Jessica, dear," Dorothy said, hobbling up to me and patting my arm. "You're doing so well. We all have complete faith in you."

"Thank you, Dorothy," I said.

"And isn't it exciting?" She giggled and I looked at her, eyebrows raised. "I've always wanted to be involved in something like this," she continued with a little shrug. "Always sounds like such fun in books, don't you agree?"

"Er . . . yeah, sure," I replied, unsure what to think.

"What are we supposed to do now?" Mr. Wallis asked.

"Sit back and enjoy the rest of the trip. There's still plenty to see and, believe me, the further we go, the more beautiful it gets."

"You said he'd been poisoned," someone else called out, and I cursed myself for having said those words out loud. "You really expect us to relax after that?"

"We don't know that for certain," I said. "He may have had an allergic reaction to something."

"Sounds to me like you're just making excuses. How can we possibly know we're safe?"

I turned toward the soft voice to find Dani leaning against the doorway. Her smile seemed so at odds with her words, but fear did funny things to people.

"I can assure you—"

84

"What she means is," Vanessa said, coming to my side, "it's free drinks all round!"

"I . . . what?" I turned to her, eyebrows raised in surprise.

"Just go with it," she muttered from the side of her mouth.

"But—"

"You'll see," she said.

"How do we know there's nothing in it? If there's a poisoner on the loose—"

Vanessa rolled her eyes. "We'll open fresh bottles. You *do* want free drinks, don't you?"

That seemed to do the trick, as the fearful whispers quickly turned into nodded agreement. Just then, I noticed Dani slipping away, back into the first carriage.

"But, Ness," I whispered at her. "We can't do that. You heard Greg say how much this trip is already costing us. What about the profits?"

"Profits schmofits," she said, still smiling at the passengers but talking to me through the side of her mouth. "We've got to do something, and future profits will amount to nothing if Gold Dust Railways gets a reputation for being Murder Express!"

CHAPTER 12

*B*efore long, everyone was back in their seats, happily sipping their free drinks. It always surprised me, people's capacity to forget and act like nothing untoward had happened.

As humans, we adapt so easily.

Especially when free alcohol is involved.

There were some sour faces, however—Beverly Lyonel's being one, and Carter's once I thanked him for his help but told him I wouldn't require anything more of him. Mr. and Mrs. Wallis seemed to be chatting happily, though, having befriended another couple, and Dorothy seemed in a world of her own, watching people in the same way I was with a mix of serenity and sincerity on her face.

Could she know something?

What with her bird-watching skills, we already knew her to be observant—she could spot the tiniest creature miles out into the forest. Surely, she could see when a murderer was in her midst too. I watched her for a moment longer, though what I was looking for I couldn't say. A clue, I supposed.

"Listen," I said, pulling my gaze away from her and turning to Vanessa. "I'm going over to the office. There's no cell reception, but there's one of those old CB radios. Greg had Lucas use it earlier, I'm sure of it. I'll call and make sure the paramedics meet us at the station, along with the police."

"I'll get into the kitchen and help the girls with the cleanup, then," Vanessa said. "Good luck!"

I would have said I didn't need luck, but the way things were going it seemed more and more likely that I would. So much for no one else getting hurt. I think we at least managed to calm the chaos, though. As I strode through the train toward the office, I smiled politely but refused to get pulled into conversation. I was more determined than ever to catch this killer, and every single one of them was a suspect.

"Hey, Lucas," I called, spotting him just as he was entering the office. "How is he?"

"Who?" Lucas asked.

"You're not serious?" Of all the stupid things I'd heard that day, this had to top the lot. Lucas couldn't really be that daft, could he? From his blank, questioning expression, I had to conclude that, yes, he was indeed that daft. "Greg!"

"Oh!" He laughed uneasily, and I hoped it was at his own foolishness. "He's sleeping. Seems a bit out of it if you ask me. Like, confused. He'll be all right, though, yeah?"

"Yeah, he'll be all right," I reassured him. "He just needs time for whatever it is to flush out of his system, and the sleep will do him good. But it's best he gets proper medical attention when we stop—I only know the basics. Speaking of which, I was hoping to use the radio to call it through. There's no cell reception here, and I know from experience that it doesn't pick up again until we're almost at the station."

"There's a code," Lucas said.

"What do you mean?"

"A security code. You've got to tap it in to get the radio to work. You know, to stop just anyone from using it. It's meant only for emergencies."

"This is an emergency," I reminded him.

"Yes, but . . . the code," he repeated.

Exasperation didn't even begin to cover what I was feeling right then. I'm sure Greg had a good reason for hiring this boy, but I couldn't see it right then.

"So, what's the code?" I asked.

"That's just it. I don't know the code. Only Greg knows the code."

I frowned at him. "Didn't he ask you to radio through to the authorities with Walter's death?" I asked. "Telling them to meet us at the station?"

He studiously avoided my eye and shifted from foot to foot. He couldn't look more uneasy, nor obviously suspicious, if he tried.

"What is it, Lucas?"

"It's just I . . . I don't know the code," he said, still not looking at me. He turned and walked into the office and I followed, closing the door behind us quietly.

"But there's more, isn't there?" He looked at me with pleading eyes and I shook my head in amazement. "For goodness' sake, Lucas! One man is dead, another is in the infirmary, there's no cell reception, we're in the middle of nowhere, and we have an hour to go before we enter any sort of civilization! I suggest you tell me everything you know right away."

Lucas huffed and sat heavily in Greg's seat, burying his face in his hands. "Fine," he said. "I forgot the code."

"What?!"

The word was loud, ringing out through the room and probably halfway down the corridor, and I gaped at Lucas. No wonder he was being so shifty.

"You can't be serious," I said. "Why didn't you just ask Greg?"

Lucas bowed his head in shame.

Oddly enough, I didn't have even an ounce of suspicion about Lucas. He was just a gawky kid, still learning the ropes and now stuck in this horrible position. If anything, I'd been a little harsh on him.

"I-I . . ." He stuttered, turning his head to look at me from under his brows. "Uh. . . ." He paused, looking up at me with his jaw working but no words coming out.

I sighed.

"Come on, Lucas. You've got nothing to worry about it. We'll protect you, if that's what's bothering you. No one else is going to get hurt."

"I don't know." He shrugged. "I . . . he's my boss. I didn't want to let him down. I worked hard to get this job, and I don't want to lose it."

I groaned into my hands. This was getting worse and worse.

"I'm sorry, Jessica, I really am."

I wasn't going to get anything else from Lucas, I knew that.

"All right. Listen, I've got to get back to the kitchen," I said. "As soon as Greg wakes up, get that code from him. Got it?"

Lucas nodded.

"I'm serious, Lucas. This is important."

"Yeah," he said. "I've got it."

* * *

"Hey, stranger," Vanessa said as soon as I walked back into the kitchen. "What a day, huh?"

Penny was at the sink. The used pots and pans were piled haphazardly beside her as she rinsed off the plates, handing them one at a time to Amy, who stacked them into the washer. Poor Amy looked exhausted, and I wasn't surprised. She always took everything to heart.

"Everything all right?" she asked. "Did you manage to call for the paramedics?"

"No, I didn't," I said through gritted teeth. "Quite the opposite. Turns out Lucas didn't call the authorities either."

"Oh," Vanessa replied. "I figured that grim expression must be for something."

Penny looked up from the dishes, a look of alarm on her young face. "Why didn't Lucas call?"

I bit my lip. I didn't want to break Lucas' confidence, especially with Penny. I shrugged. "He needs the code from Greg," I said. "As for Greg, he's still sleeping, but as soon as he's well enough, we'll get the code." I sighed. "You know, I've had an odd feeling about Greg all day."

"Greg?" Vanessa asked, clearly shocked. "No way. He's been helping with the investigation!"

"And controlling it," I reminded her. "Perhaps it was just his way of keeping an eye on us. It was inevitable someone was going to find Walter, and by acting like he was desperate to find the killer, Greg made it look like he was innocent. He has motive, remember?"

"Yeah, but he did tell us his motive himself," Amy reasoned. "It wasn't like he was trying to hide the fact that he was angry at Walter. He wanted us to know because he was worried about being blamed."

"Isn't that what you would do if you had killed someone?" I asked. "Think about it. It's a clever way of redirecting someone's attention."

"But Greg never could," Penny said, shaking her head. "His bark is pretty bad at times, but he's not a murderer."

"He's a pussy cat, even," Vanessa said. "You saw how messed up he was earlier on. I swear I saw him shaking at one point. You can't fake that kind of shock."

"I'm not saying he killed Walter on purpose," I said, falling back against the countertop and sighing. "But maybe there was some sort of . . . I don't know, fight between them, and it was an accident. And if you'd just accidentally killed someone, wouldn't you be in pretty bad shock? Shaking and everything?"

"All right, all right," Vanessa said, hands in the air. "Even if we were to go with your crazy theory, you're forgetting one major thing."

"What's that?" I asked.

"He was poisoned!" She laughed without humor, shaking her head at me as though I was crazy.

"Not badly though," I said.

Vanessa almost choked. "How can it not be bad? He was poisoned!"

"What I mean is he's fine—or he will be. The poison didn't affect him that badly, did it?"

"Where did he get the poison if this whole thing was an accident?" she asked.

I shrugged again. That was one flaw in my theory. Unless . . . I gasped. "Unless he faked the whole thing! He wasn't poisoned at all, just pretended to be."

"There ain't no actor in the world who's that good," Vanessa said, scoffing. "The color of his skin changed!"

"Hmmm, yeah." I put a finger to my lips and stared at the floor.

Vanessa was right about that. "Maybe he has some sort of allergy then. One that he knows about and—"

"I think you're clutching at straws," Vanessa said.

"No, listen. Hear me out." They were all looking at me as though I'd lost my mind. "He's got motive, right? And means. No one would have questioned him being in the motorcar or talking with Walter." I was counting out my points on my fingers as I spoke.

"Still doesn't—" Amy said.

"He wanted to stop the train, then he didn't want to stop the train, like he was just going with whatever everyone else said to stop the suspicion."

"But—" Vanessa said.

"And the shock you mentioned?" I said. "That's another pointer. He was in a right state until we agreed to help, taking the heat off him. He almost instantly calmed, probably because we were focusing our attentions on other people. And he's been pretty insistent about Beverly Lyonel, hasn't he?"

"That's true," Vanessa conceded, cocking her head in my direction. "But she does have a habit of making herself look guilty."

"Yes, but I don't think she is. She's just a strong woman. Why does everyone always blame the strong woman?" They all nodded in agreement at that. They'd all been in that situation before. "Listen, our killer must be pretty smart, right? And what's smarter than telling everyone why you did it while pretending you didn't? And then making yourself look like a victim, too! He was throwing us off the scent, and he could do that purely *because* he was helping with the investigation."

The kitchen fell silent. Even Penny and Amy stopped clattering dishes.

"Well, you make a good case," Vanessa conceded eventually. "But you don't really believe all that, do you?"

I paused, asking myself that very question.

Did I?

Part of me did. It made sense. But the other part of me kept saying the same thing over and over: *but it's Greg*! And apart from Vanessa, I'd known Greg longer than anyone else on this train. If it *was* him, I at least knew he would not have done it maliciously, assuming it's possible to murder anyone without malice. If he did do it, it would have been an accident, and he panicked and tried to cover it up.

That didn't make it right though.

"Jessica? What are you thinking?" Vanessa asked.

"Oh, I don't know." I stared out of the window, the beautiful countryside speeding past. "Yes and no. I don't know what to believe. It all makes so much sense, but there's something in my head that's stopping me from thinking we've solved this case."

"Yeah, I get what you're saying," Vanessa said. "But I think that means that's not the answer. You've got great instincts, Jessica, always have had. Trust them."

She was right. I had to follow my gut. And my gut told me there was more we didn't know.

"At least Walter didn't need feeding. Greg had a full meal before he went down!" Penny said after a pause, a snort of laughter coming from her lips.

"Don't be so heartless," I said, shaking my head at her in astonishment.

She was not normally one to be so cruel, nor so crass. I didn't meet her gaze, but I tilted my head and watched her surreptitiously. It was such an odd thing to say, and though she probably said it out of unease, it still didn't sit right with me.

"I wonder who's next," she said then, and I couldn't stop myself scowling. What had got into her?

"Let's not think like that, shall we?" I said, though I think we were all secretly wondering the same thing. No one would be next if I had my way. Whoever it was—even if it was Greg—had gone too far already.

Just then, the train lurched again. I gasped and threw my hand out to steady myself as the train slowed to a stop. We weren't stationary for long, it being less than a minute before the train pulled off again, but it was long enough for us all to know something was wrong. That wasn't the normal jerk and pull of the train's movement.

"Not again," Amy moaned.

"Guess we'll find out sooner than we thought," Penny said.

"It can't possibly be, can it?" I asked, looking at each of them in turn.

Vanessa threw me a worried look, but she said, "I'll go find out what happened."

"Thanks, Ness," I said as she left. I sat on her stool—it would always be her stool now—and I looked out of the window.

The forest was my favorite, but the mountains were a close second. They were so isolated and peaceful, so far away from the rest of the world—and normally that was a good thing, even if today it had been a bit of a hindrance. I looked forward to seeing them in winter, with their snow-topped peaks. Having lived in the area my whole life, I knew they were beautiful no matter the season, but seeing them from the train did give a unique perspective, and working here allowed me to admire them all year round. I really did have the perfect job, especially when there wasn't a murderer on board and everyone was safe.

"Are you two all right finishing the cleanup?" I asked.

"I'd rather be in here than out there," Amy said. "What with everything that's gone on. And it's nothing we can't handle, is it, Penny?"

"Nope," Penny replied with a smile. "You know how much I love doing dishes!"

"But you like to moan more," I said with a chuckle as I got up from my seat.

I jumped when I opened the kitchen door. There was Dani, loitering just outside. I inhaled sharply, my skin tingling with discomfort. Of all the days to sneak up on people! Today was not a day for surprises.

"Dani," I managed on a gasp. "How can I help?"

"I'm sorry," she said, smiling awkwardly but with a creased brow. "I didn't mean to make you jump."

"No, it's all right," I said, laughing at myself. "Is there something the matter?"

"No," she said. "I was just wondering how the manager was? Such an awful thing to witness. I really hope he's doing okay."

"He is, thank you," I said, smiling at her kindness. "He'll need proper medical attention, but I think we got to him in time."

"Thank goodness," she said. "I know it's silly, but I hate the idea of anyone being hurt."

"It's not silly at all, Dani," I said.

She smiled at me, and she continued smiling as she turned to leave. She glanced over her shoulder at me as she went through the far door and back to her seat, and it was then I thought I saw it. I couldn't be certain, but . . .

Did she just scowl?

CHAPTER 13

efore I had time to fully think it through, Mr. and Mrs. Wallis popped up in front of me.

"Amazing show," Mr. Wallis said, looking suitably impressed.

I blinked at him. "Show?" I asked.

"We'd heard so much about this trip," Mrs. Wallis said over his shoulder. "But no one mentioned just how exciting the entertainment is."

"Entertainment?" I asked, eyebrow raised and with absolutely no idea what they were talking about.

"The whole murder mystery thing," Mr. Wallis said. "We've heard about those sorts of parties before, and I've always liked the idea of it. But we didn't realize this was one of them."

"Oh," I said. "That." Now that *was* a surprise. There I was, worried the passengers would be in a panic, when at least some of them thought it all a game.

"Do we all get to have a guess of *whodunit?*" Mrs. Wallis asked with a squeal of glee. "Is there a prize?"

Other than putting a murderer in jail? I thought.

"The actors you hired were so good. I would never have guessed in a million years," Mr. Wallis laughed.

"Yeah," I said—slowly to allow myself time to think. "Yeah, they're an amazing bunch. You've got until the end of the trip to work it out."

"Ooh . . . how exciting," Mrs. Wallis said.

I smiled and started to turn away, but as I did, I had an idea. "Say, if you get any clues or theories, let me know, won't you? I may be able to offer a few pointers."

I winked at them as though I was doing them a favor, then walked away in complete and utter astonishment.

At least they're not frightened!

In many ways, it would be better if everyone believed it to be just a bit of entertainment—for now, at least.

And they may even help me find an answer to all this!

I'd tell them the truth once we were stationed; they deserved that much, and I was sure they'd understand.

When I left the kitchen, I didn't really know where I was going, I didn't have a plan. So I meandered through the train until I came to Dorothy. I knew she'd stop me for a chat; she always did.

"Jessica dear," she said, beaming at me. "I am simply so impressed with how you handled all that mess earlier on."

"Thank you, Dorothy. That's really kind of you to say."

"I'm not at all surprised something happened to him, you know," she whispered conspiratorially.

I frowned at her. "No? Why's that?"

She tutted. "Such a nosey parker, isn't he? He's been asking everyone all sorts of questions today. No tact or sophistication like you have, my dear." She put a warm hand on my forearm. "It was only a matter of time before he came down with something."

"Bit extreme though, isn't it?" I asked. "Poisoning someone for being nosey?"

"Poison?" Her hand flew to her chest and shook her head at me. "My, my, dear. I meant karma. Do you think . . . No, it's not possible, is it? Why would anybody want to do such a thing?"

I laughed in a poor attempt at disguising my discomfort. "No, of course not, Dorothy. Ignore me. It's been a stressful day and I can't help jumping to conclusions."

"Ah, good," she said, seemingly satisfied by my answer. "Although now you mention it . . ."

"What?" I asked, perhaps a little quicker than necessary.

"If someone *did* slip something into his drink—not that I'm saying they did—it wouldn't have been all that difficult. He was far too busy gossiping and often left his drink unattended. I'm sure I even saw him pick up someone else's once or twice. Just think, dear. It could have been any of us!"

"It could have been," I agreed with a solemn nod.

"What are you two whispering about?" Carter asked.

"Nothing to do with you," Dorothy said haughtily.

"Yet more evidence that something shifty is going on," he said. "Especially after what happened to poor Greg."

I sighed. I didn't want to be caught up in the middle of their bickering. "Thank you for your help, Carter," I said, hoping to change the subject. "We're all very grateful."

"It's nice to finally be allowed to assist you in something. Perhaps in the future there will be other ways in which I can help. I have great knowledge about these trains, you know, and this one in particular."

"I will insist on it, Carter."

He grinned proudly, clearly feeling as though he had achieved something or been finally recognized.

At least someone was happy!

Perhaps all Carter ever wanted was to be part of a team. I know that, more than once, he'd asked Greg for a job and been turned down. He might even have a chance now that we were at least one employee down. I wondered how good Carter was with computers and whether he would become our next techy genius.

"Hey, you," Vanessa said, coming through the door at the other end of the train.

"Hey," I said. She didn't *look* like anyone else had died, so that was a positive. "Any news on what happened?"

"That kid in charge—Lucas, is it? He said it was a technical fault, but that all seems to be working fine again now."

"Technical fault?"

Vanessa shrugged. "That's what he said."

I was confused. There were never any technical faults. The

majority of the train was run off mechanics that seemed unlikely to cause the train to lurch and stop, even for a few seconds. It wasn't that easy to make a steam train stop; as long as there was steam, there was movement. No, there was definitely more to this, no matter what Lucas or anyone else said.

"That's just what everyone says when they don't know, isn't it?" I said. "Or when they're trying to cover something up. Come on, let's get somewhere quieter so we can work out what's going on."

"Good idea," Vanessa said. "Kitchen?"

"No. Let's go the other way. The corridor near the bathrooms seems like a safe bet."

She looked at me curiously, and I avoided her gaze. I didn't want to tell her the truth: that I was wary of talking more in front of Penny, even while I knew, without a shadow of a doubt, that she had nothing to do with this. I don't know where that feeling came from, but I followed it. I had to if I wanted any chance of finding a solution to this mystery. Like Vanessa said, I had to trust my instinct, even if that instinct was only to protect my team from further trauma.

"All right," she said, looking at me strangely but saying no more about it. "Anyway, listen, I've had the strangest feeling."

"Oh yeah?"

"I'm sure someone's been following me round the carriages."

"You've seen someone?" I asked her back as we moved down the aisle.

"Not seen, as such," she admitted. "Just a feeling I get. And like, dark shadows that seem to move, like someone's jumped out of the way before I got a proper look at them. Does that make sense?"

"Sure does," I said as we stepped into the quiet carriage. I was pleased to be out of the way of the passengers and their noise, and I leant against the wall, pulling Vanessa next to me.

"Do you think someone could have been following me?" Vanessa asked. "Or is it just paranoia?"

"I don't know. I feel like everyone's watching me too. Like they all know what's going on and can see what I'm thinking."

"That's it exactly!" Vanessa said excitedly. "Maybe it isn't just me, then."

I shrugged.

"It's probably normal in a situation like this," Vanessa said.

I snorted. "Is there a normal when it comes to situations like this? I tell you, I've been thinking the craziest things. I even doubted Penny for a moment back there!"

"Penny? Now you are talking crazy," Vanessa said, and she was right.

"Yeah. I love a good puzzle as much as the next guy, but I sure am glad I'm not a detective. I bet they feel like that all the time."

"Nah, they probably get used to it."

"Maybe."

This carriage was the quietest of them all, with Greg's office at the far end, taking the right-hand windows. The infirmary was just opposite us, the windows to the left, and the facilities were in the middle. The corridor curved in a shallow s-shape, leading onto the motorcar ahead, and the whole place had less of a luxury feeling than the rest of the train. The windows were hung with simple blinds and the floor was covered in a standard linoleum.

People rarely came here, so was I'm not surprised the killer got in without anyone noticing. Unless it really was Mrs. Lyonel, of course.

"Do you think it was the same person? Who killed Walter and tried to kill Greg, I mean?"

I shrugged. "I suppose that would be the logical conclusion," I said. "Though Dorothy said something interesting. She told me Greg had a habit of picking up the wrong glass."

"You think maybe the poison wasn't meant for him, but someone else?" she asked.

"I don't think so," I replied with a shake of my head. "My gut tells me it was meant for Greg all along."

I turned to look out of the window. Vanessa copied my movements and, together, we stared out at the verdant hills as we talked.

"Why?" she asked. I could see Vanessa's reflection in the glass. She had a look of pure concentration on her face.

"Whoever did it would be keeping an eye on that drink, wouldn't you think?"

"Depends on whether they were targeting a specific person, or just enjoying the drama of poisoning someone—anyone."

"Again," I said, frowning at the outside world. "I don't see that. It if was someone who enjoyed killing for the sake of it, they'd have a preferred method, wouldn't they?"

Vanessa winced at the thought. "Do we have to get into the gruesome details?" she asked.

"I'm serious. Hear me out. The killer comes on board with a single target, right? He has enough poison to do just that. But then something happens . . . someone gets in the way or something. I don't know. Some brawl or something, and someone gets stabbed, because the killer only has enough poison for one."

"Hmmm . . . I don't know," Vanessa replied, but the more I thought of it, the more it made sense.

"Maybe there isn't a connection between the two after all," I said. "What reason would someone have to kill Walter *and* Greg? What's the connection?"

"They both work for Gold Dust Railways?" Vanessa ventured.

"Yeah, I thought of that. But why them in particular?"

"Could be someone with a grudge against the company and is looking for a way to make them pay," Vanessa said. "Kill a few of the staff, get the news out there, ruin the business."

"Right," I said, considering her suggestion. It was a good one. "Maybe we need to look at a list of staff that's been recently laid off."

Vanessa frowned. "But Gold Dust Railways is hiring right now. I mean they hired you only a couple months ago. I can't think of anyone disgruntled or laid off, can you?"

I shrugged. "Not off the top of my head. And really knowing the morbid way the general public thinks, murders on the train would likely *increase* sales, not reduce them, don't you think?"

Vanessa snorted. "You're probably right. Gold Dust would turn it into a marketing opportunity. Tourists would want to see where the great railway murders took place."

"Exactly. No, I think it's more likely that Walter—or maybe Greg too—were just in the wrong place at the wrong time, not that they were both targeted."

"You should ask that Carter fella," Vanessa said. "He seems to know everything."

"All the regulars do," I said with a shrug. "Carter just vocalizes it more than anyone else. You think he's got motive?"

"He could have been trying to tell Walter what to do and when Walter refused, a fight ensued."

"Just like Beverly Lyonel arguing with him? Unlikely, don't you think?"

"What if Beverly was trying to headhunt him for her own business and when he said no, she punished him? She seems like the type to insist on getting her own way, and I bet when she doesn't, there's hell to pay."

"Okay. Interesting idea. But if either of those scenarios were true," I said, "why would they go on to try to kill Greg, as well?"

"Yeah, that bit's a little more complicated," she admitted with a twist of her lips. "Dorothy wasn't happy about the changes made to the meal," she added quickly. "That would give her motive to kill Walter *and* Greg."

I laughed. "I hardly think dissatisfaction about the menu is a motive to kill, is it?"

"Is for some people, I guess." She shrugged. "You hear of people killed for less on the news."

"No way. I don't believe it. Too unlikely for me."

"Who else is on the list, then? What about Lucas? He might have wanted to take Greg's job."

"He's way too young and inexperienced for a chance at Greg's job. And what about Walter?" I asked before laughing. "Somehow he just doesn't seem capable to me."

"Ah, but there's his ploy . . ." She turned to me and wiggled her eyebrows. "But I suppose you're right. He looks terrified just at the prospect of coming into the kitchen."

I tutted and nudged her playfully. We were coming out of the mountains now, the landscape opening up around us. There was nothing for miles around, just pure bliss and untouched nature.

"I told you about that Dani, didn't I?" I said.

"The small one with the bad attitude?"

"That's her. She came to the kitchen to ask how Greg is doing."

"Bit weird," she said. "But what if she genuinely was concerned?"

"When she's had such an attitude with me up until now?"

Vanessa snorted. "We've both had teenagers in the house, Jessica. You know full well a bad attitude doesn't make you a killer, and we've all experienced those sorts of mood swings."

"She's not a teenager though," I said.

"True. Maybe she just doesn't like you then."

"You can be cruel sometimes," I said with a laugh. "You know everybody likes me!"

"Yeah, actually, I do," she said. "So what do we know so far?"

"Not a lot. You know, I'm still convinced there's a connection between the two. Walter and Greg, I mean. It would be far too much of a coincidence otherwise, wouldn't it? Two murderers on the same train?"

"Assuming Greg actually *was* poisoned. We won't know that for sure until he's seen a professional," Vanessa said.

"You don't really believe that, do you?" I asked. "I mean, I know I suggested it, but I'm not sure even I agree with it."

"No, of course not," she said, shaking her head. "I think you're right. Assuming Greg didn't poison himself—which I'm pretty sure he didn't, even though you made such a good case for it—there must be some reason someone would want them both dead."

"And in different ways." We paused, both pursing our lips as we watched the hills flatten out. I met her eyes in our reflection. "I think we need to go and see Greg."

Vanessa nodded her agreement, and the two of us turned. The infirmary was just behind us, though the door was on the shorter wall, perpendicular to the train. I knocked gently, wanting to speak to him but also not wanting to disturb him. There was no answer.

"You don't think he's . . . you know . . . do you?" Vanessa asked.

"What?" I asked. "Dead?" I tried to laugh off the idea, but she was right. The silence was worrying.

I tried again, but this time when there was no answer, I twisted the door handle and let myself in. As the first-aider, I had a right, didn't I?

"Hey, Greg," I said quietly. "We were just . . . oh!"

The bed was empty. Greg was gone.

CHAPTER 14

e shared a worried look, and I swallowed before turning back to the empty infirmary bed. The sheets had been disturbed, and there was a dent from his head on the pillow, so he had definitely been there at some point. But now, he was not.

"He's not here," Vanessa said.

"Thanks for that," I said, turning to her with a wry smile. "I would never have guessed."

"But . . . where is he?"

I looked at her, my lips pressed together and my eyes wide. My whole body felt heavy with the weight of this new revelation, my heart sinking at the realization that yet another thing had gone wrong. I had no idea where Greg could possibly be. And it could only mean one of two things: the killer came back for round two, or it was him after all and he'd made his escape.

I looked around the small room in some vain hope I'd find a clue or, even better, Greg hidden in some corner. Funny, the things hope leads us to believe. The infirmary only took up about a quarter of a coach, maybe a little bit more. The bed was tucked against the wall, next to a window that had blinds pulled all the way down. On the other side was a locked cupboard with some basic medical supplies and equipment. I ran my fingertips over the bed, frowning as I looked around.

There was nothing. No clues. It didn't look like there'd been a struggle, making me think that perhaps no killer had come after him at all. But then, he was weakened. The last time I saw him, he could hardly stand on his own, and who knew what state he was in now. If someone had come to take him, chances are there wouldn't have been a struggle at all.

"You think he's done a runner?" Vanessa asked, as easily as if she was asking me if I thought it was going to rain.

"And gone where? He can't get off the train."

She shrugged. "No, that's true, but he could hide on it somewhere. I have no doubt there are plenty of closets and corners where someone could hide out until the time came for them to make their escape. We should send some people out to look."

"I don't know," I replied, sitting down on the bed. "Who are we going to send? And even if he is the killer—which is a big *if*—and if he did poison himself to put us off the scent, why would he run away now? His ruse was a success, wasn't it?"

"Maybe he overheard you talking in the corridor," Greg said from the doorway, "and knew the game was up. You've got me dead to rights."

"Greg!" I jumped up and looked at him, choking back my surprise. "Where have you been?"

He was holding himself up against the doorframe. His eyes seemed hollowed out, deep with dark circles beneath them, and his lips were still pale, the color not quite returned to them in the same way it had his cheeks. He was clearly a lot better than he had been, but he still had a way to go.

I didn't know if I was happy to see him or not. Annoyed, certainly, but that was nothing new when it came to Greg. At least he hadn't been captured by some sadistic madman, and he wasn't in hiding. He had made us worry, though, and this was hardly the first thing he'd done wrong that day.

"I needed to use the facilities," he said. "That is allowed, isn't it?"

"Ugh!" Vanessa let out a snort of annoyance that I could completely relate to. "You had us worried, you idiot!"

He rolled his eyes, then half walked, half staggered to the bed, falling heavily onto it with a sigh.

"I heard you talking when I was on my way to the bathroom. I'm glad to know you've ruled me out of your inquiries," he said, lying back and looking up at the ceiling. "Although I must admit I was a little disappointed to find myself on your list in the first place. You don't really think I'd be capable of murder, do you?"

I shook my head, shifting uncomfortably, but I defended myself all the same. He had no right to enlist me into this and then question me. And it was his own fault!

"If you hadn't been acting so suspiciously, we would never have considered you," I said, glaring down at him. "And yes, actually. I think we're all capable of murder in our own way."

"And you've got motive," Vanessa said.

"Yeah, thanks. I can see that now. Look, you know it wasn't me, don't you? Please tell me you know it wasn't me."

"Yes," I said, although in truth there was still a tiny seed of doubt. Not enough to stop us investigating anyone else, but just enough to stop me from fully trusting him. "What's the code for the radio?"

He frowned. "The code? I gave it to Lucas. What are you on about?"

"Listen, I don't want to get anyone in trouble. Just tell me the code."

"Are you saying that the person I gave the code to—"

"Greg!"

"Okay, okay." He held his hands up in submission. "Eight, nine, two, four."

"Thank you." I glanced over to Vanessa and nodded. She knew exactly what I was saying.

"I'll go tell Lucas," she said. "Get him to phone it through."

"Ambulance, too. Don't forget," I called to her retreating back.

"Yeah, yeah."

"Ambulance?" Greg asked once she'd left, his forehead wrinkled with worry. "What's that for? Has someone else been hurt?"

"Wow, that stuff really got to your brain as well as your body, huh?" I said. "It's for you, obviously. You were poisoned, Greg. I did what I could, but you need to be checked over by a professional."

"I'm perfectly fine now, Jessie," he said, sitting up and taking a sip of water. He sounded almost tired of it all. "I've vomited a few times. Seems to have done the trick. All I need now is a bit of sleep."

"You don't *look* perfectly fine," I said. "You look like you've ingested something you shouldn't have. It's clearly not affected you too badly, but I'd feel much better if you—"

"Careful, Jessie," he said, cocking his head in that arrogant way of his. Yeah, he was returning to normal.

"What?"

"If you're not careful, I'll start thinking you care."

"Don't go thinking that; you'd be so wrong," I said, folding my arms across my chest. I pursed my lips, doing everything I could to stop them from twisting into a smile.

He didn't deserve a smile, at least not yet, no matter how much I enjoyed the banter.

"I want to know whether I was right to give you the charcoal, and only a professional can tell us that."

"Yeah," he said, looking down at his hands. He seemed solemn all of a sudden, sincere. No longer mocking and irritating, like he remembered what a serious situation we were in. "About that. The charcoal or whatever it was. Listen, thank you." He sounded uneasy, like thanking someone was not something he was used to. "I'm incredibly grateful. You saved my life, Jessie."

"Don't get too comfortable," I teased. "I might kill you myself if you do something stupid like calling me Jessie again. It's Jessica."

He smiled at me, and I could see the laughter building behind his lips. *Idiot.*

"I know," he said with a half sigh that irritated me more than a full sigh would. "The thing is, you look so cute when you're all riled up. I can't help myself."

Wow. I jutted my chin out, refusing to look at him.

"You are quite possibly the most infuriating man I have ever met, Greg Kendrick."

I jumped around when I heard someone clear their throat behind me. I had the odd feeling that I had been caught out doing something I shouldn't, but that was nuts. I certainly wasn't doing something I shouldn't have.

"Not interrupting anything, am I?" she sang as she entered the room. Vanessa, just in time to save me.

"Nothing to interrupt," I said. "Call made?"

She nodded. "He called them while I was there. They advised that Greg shouldn't eat or drink anything other than water, in case it reacts with whatever he was given. Got it, Greg?"

"As if I'd even want to right now," he said, feigning a nauseous expression.

"As for the other matter . . ." Vanessa trailed off, looking at me for reassurance she could talk in front of Greg. I offered her the tiniest nod, telling her it was all right.

"The small matter of the murder investigation, you mean?" I asked.

"That's it," she said. She shifted awkwardly, like she didn't want to tell us the next bit. "They told us to do our best to keep everyone calm, but not to investigate it ourselves or detain anyone, as we're not professionals and we might unintentionally cause harm to ourselves or others."

The three of us fell silent, looking at each other with that silent question—whether or not we were going to do what we were told.

The tension stabbed at me. I wanted to do what the authorities told us, and yet . . . I almost laughed. I hadn't wanted to get involved in this case, but now that I had, the puzzle of it had wormed its way into me and I wouldn't—I couldn't—let it drop.

"We're not going to listen to them, are we?" Greg asked, looking rapidly from me to Vanessa.

No, we're not.

"Too right we're not," Vanessa said, and they both looked at me.

"No," I agreed. "I'm far too invested in this now. I need to find out the truth."

Greg grinned. "I knew you would be hooked once you got going. You're a sucker for a good mystery!"

I rolled my eyes at him. Trust him to take the credit for everything.

"I just love how seriously you're taking all this, Greg. Doesn't it bother you that Walter is dead or that someone tried to kill you?"

"Of course it does," he said. "And I *am* taking it seriously. I'm just pleased to have you working on it with me. Is that such a bad thing? I think I can have both those feelings." When I didn't answer him, he continued. "All right then, let's get down to business. What have you found out so far?"

"Not a lot," Vanessa admitted with a grimace. She hunched her shoulders, looking almost ashamed, but I wished she didn't. Murder investigations took more than a couple of hours, and we were doing well, considering none of us had a minute's experience.

"Anything at all?" Greg ventured.

"Actually, we were hoping you might have some answers," I said quickly. "Like who might have wanted to poison you and who had access to your drink."

"I don't know, and I don't know," Greg said. "That's a negative on both counts."

"Well, you're about as useful as a candle without a wick," Vanessa said. She rubbed the back of her neck, rolling her shoulders to release the tension. I knew how she felt. A massage right then wouldn't have gone amiss.

"Why would anyone want to kill me?" he asked, his voice high-pitched with disbelief. "I'm wonderful!"

"I could list about ten reasons," I muttered.

"I was hardly keeping an eye on my glass," Greg said, more serious this time and evidently ignoring my dig. "Everybody on the train would have had an opportunity at one point or another. Motive's a bit more difficult. I might joke around, and I know I can be annoying, but I genuinely can't think of a reason someone would want me dead."

"Dorothy said people were getting irritated by your questioning," I said, but Greg shook his head.

"I didn't sense that at all."

"Reading people's emotions never has been your strong point," I said. "Even in a professional capacity."

"Perhaps not," he conceded, looking sheepishly at me. "I do try, though, Jessica. I really do. I'm not as bad as you think."

We shared a moment, looking at each other, but I quickly turned away. This wasn't about any of that, and it certainly wasn't about any of the difficulties Greg and I had had over the past weeks.

"Do you personally know anyone on the train?" Vanessa asked, and I silently thanked her for interrupting.

Greg looked at the floor, slowly shaking his head. "No. I don't think so. Other than the regulars, of course." He looked back up at us. "There was that one woman. You remember the one, Jessica?"

Vanessa looked questioningly at me. "He means Dani."

"Oh," she said.

"You met her?"

"A few times," I said. "You remember where you know her from now?"

"No. I've seen her before, I'm sure of it. I just . . . I just can't put my finger on where from. It's maddening."

"I'm still going with scorned lover," I said with a chuckle. "She came to the kitchen asking after your health not long after we brought you here."

"Sweet," he said, raising an eyebrow. "She cares."

"Or she was hoping you were dead," Vanessa said with a snort. "As I imagine all of your ex-girlfriends do."

"Wow," he said. "Harsh."

"Maybe," I snorted, "but—"

The train lurched yet again, stopping our conversation in its tracks, and we were plunged into darkness.

CHAPTER 15

"Well, I wasn't expecting that," I said, looking up at the dead light bulb in the ceiling as Greg fumbled with the blind. It rolled up noisily and snapped against the frame at the top, making us all jump, but at least allowing the sunlight to flood into the room.

"What's happened now?" Vanessa asked.

"No doubt another technical fault," I muttered. "Let's go check it out."

"Good idea," Greg said, getting off the bed.

"Not you," I snapped, though a little harsher than I had intended. Exasperation does that to a person. "You stay in bed. You still need to rest. We've got this under control. Seriously, Greg, how many times do I have to tell you?"

He glared at me as though he was about to defy my orders, but with a raised eyebrow from me, he quickly gave in. "Fine."

I opened the door to the infirmary, and the screams that had been muffled by the walls grew louder, more pronounced. They weren't screams of fear, as such. More of confusion, panic perhaps.

"What's happening?" Vanessa asked behind me. "They freaking out because of the lights?"

"Hopefully that's all it is," I said. "You go see if you can calm them. I'm going to the motorcar."

"But Walter—"

"I know," I said. I didn't want to think about that. I'd already decided I would skip through the car as quickly as I could. I was neither as bold nor as curious as Vanessa. I had no desire to lift the corner of the blanket for a quick look.

The motorcar, as we knew it, was actually made up of two carriages. At the very front was the steam engine. It was a hot, noisy, messy place, where the men shoveled coal and the engine thundered. That was the vintage part of the train. Behind that was a second, smaller carriage that we always considered part of the motorcar. That's where Walter was, along with all the modern workings—the trip switches for the electric, the control units for the AC and the heating, the Wi-Fi router, all that sort of stuff. It was not as busy in there, the more up-to-date commodities running pretty much by themselves. It was still hot, though, thanks to all the machinery, and the noise of the engine was loud enough that you had to shout in the second carriage too.

Despite the panic and chaos behind me, I opened the door slowly and peered in. Though I averted my eyes, I could still see the vague shape of a body under a brown wool blanket. It was one of those itchy, uncomfortable ones you get in hospitals. *They could have given him something a bit more comfortable*, I thought, before reminding myself he wouldn't much care anymore. I reckon he'd take an itchy blanket over death any day. I forced myself to look away.

To the left, I could see Ralph, looking incredibly serious and perhaps a bit panicked as he flicked switches on the electricity board. His face was dirty from the remnants of coal and sweat, his hat perched on his head. Ahead, I could hear the roar of the engine and the shouts of the other engineers as they worked hard to keep the train moving.

"Hey," I said, stepping fully into the car, but he didn't hear me. "Hey," I said again, louder this time. "What's going on?"

"I . . .er . . ." He didn't turn to look at me but continued to stare at the switches. He pulled his hat off, scratched his head, and thrust the hat back on before huffing. "I don't know. Seems like every time our back's turned, something goes wrong."

"When your back's turned?" I asked, curious about his choice of phrasing. Technical faults, whenever they did occur, rarely cared whether someone was watching.

"Yeah," he said, still not looking at me but cocking his head to one side. "Everything works fine when we're looking at it. It's just when we're not that things go wrong, and that ain't normal, is it?"

"I suppose not," I said, frowning.

Already, the heat from the engine was seeping into me, and I blew my breath up my face in an attempt to keep cool.

This heat couldn't be good for Walter, surely?

At least we'd be stationed soon and he would be taken somewhere more appropriate. I could still see his body out of the corner of my eye. I had the weirdest feeling—like he was going to pop up suddenly, declaring it all a ruse, some stupid joke cooked up by him and Greg.

If he did that, I'd have to kill him myself—and Greg, for that matter.

But I knew he wouldn't. He was gone. It's not like Walter and I were ever particularly close. He was a work colleague, and a distant one at that. His death hit me surprisingly hard, though. I'd miss the guy and that nasally voice of his. I suppose you never truly know how you feel about a person until they're gone. With a sigh, I turned to look.

His body was sort of slumped against the wall, not lying flat on the floor as I'd imagined. I wondered whether he had fallen and died like that, or whether they'd dragged his body into the corner to give themselves more space to work. The very thought sent a shiver down my spine, and I forced myself to put it out of my head. That wasn't going to get me anywhere, and I was determined to get *somewhere*. I would do it for Walter, if for nothing else.

"Hey, Ralph? Do you think someone's coming in here, messing with everything?" I asked.

When he turned to look at me, his face was pale. His wide, haunted eyes told me that's exactly what he thought, but when he spoke, he said something different. "Certainly feels that way, what with . . ." He pointed vaguely in Walter's direction. "But can't possibly be true. Someone sneaking in and out without ever being noticed? I don't believe in no ghosts."

"No," I said. "No, I don't either."

"Look," he said. "Everyone out there is probably panicking, right? There was that thing with Greg and then the lights and everything."

"Yeah." I nodded. "Don't think there'll be any sweet-talking our way out of this one."

"Get back out there and calm everyone down," he said. "We'll get the lights back up and running as soon as possible."

"You're sure?" I asked. "Nothing I can do to help?"

"Sure as I can be. And let's just pray nothing else happens. What've we got left? Forty minutes?"

"If that," I said.

"Well then." He turned back to the switch board and frowned again. "Not much can happen in less than forty minutes, right?"

"Right."

He was so very wrong. A lot could happen in forty minutes. I just hoped it would be enough time to put an end to all this madness. We had forty minutes to keep everyone calm, forty minutes to prevent anyone else from getting hurt.

Forty minutes to catch a killer.

I turned and walked slowly from the motorcar. I paused before opening the door, taking a deep breath and forcing a smile on my face. I would do this, and I would do it by winning people over with friendliness and kindness. That was the only way they'd open up to me.

When I arrived in the first passenger car, the screams had died down, but the panic was still there, electric in the air. People were throwing questions out at each other, demanding to know what was going on. There was one man who stood on his seat, prodding the light bulb above him as though that was somehow going to help.

Didn't he see the whole lot had gone out?

Vanessa stood over the join between to the two cars, fielding inquiries from both, but from the expression on her face, I could see she was failing.

"Hey, chef lady," someone shouted, and I turned to look. "What's going on? Why have the lights gone out?"

"Just a technical difficulty, sir," I said. "Luckily, the sun is shining brightly, and we can still look out at the beautiful landscape."

"I don't want to look out at the landscape," he said firmly. "I want to know what is going on. This is supposed to be a luxury trip, but so far, very little of it has been luxurious."

"I'm sorry you feel that way. As I said, technical difficulty. The team is working on it now."

"And how's that manager doing?" someone else said, causing me to spin around. "What a mess that was!"

"He's faring well. Thank you for asking," I replied with a smile. "All he needs is a little rest."

"Do we know what happened to him?" a third person asked.

"Not yet," I admitted. "But the paramedics will be meeting us at the station, just to give him a check over."

"What about the cops?" I spun around yet again, dizzied by the shouts and cries. I felt like a hundred people wanted a piece of me, when it was supposed to be the other way around. Wasn't I the one meant to be asking the questions?

"What about them?" I asked.

"They should be there!" Another voice. "It's obvious enough to anyone with half a brain that someone slipped something into his drink."

"We don't know that," I replied as calmly as I could. "It's just as likely that Mr. Kendrick had a reaction to something, an allergy."

"Yeah, right!"

I caught Vanessa's eye and she shook her head at me. The movement was so small that no one else would have noticed, but I saw it. She was worried, drowning in a sea of panicked cries. I nodded, equally as subtly. I figured the best way to get them calm would be to leave them to it and let their questions fizzle out between themselves.

"Hey! The network's not working!" I turned to look at the young woman who had called out. She was staring down at her phone screen and scowling.

It still amazed me how many people were glued to their phones when they were in such magnificent surroundings. Don't get me wrong, I loved my phone as much as anyone, but there was a time and a place, right? It baffled me that anyone would choose to stare at a screen instead of enjoying the countryside. That's why they came on this trip in the first place. They might as well have stayed in the office if they weren't going to embrace the experience.

"I've been kicked off too!" A man, this time, with a laptop.

I frowned, looking between the two of them. This wasn't to do with Greg or the lights or the way the train kept stopping or any of it. This was a whole new problem to add to our list.

"What's wrong?" Vanessa asked, turning into the carriage and taking a step toward us.

"I've been booted off the network," the woman explained. "I was just streaming the Gold Dust featured movie and . . . bam! Network down! I thought Wi-Fi was part of the package?"

I laughed nervously, sharing a look with Vanessa. "That's normal at this point in the journey, I'm afraid," I said. "No signal for miles. Not in such isolated countryside like this."

"You can't be serious?" the man scoffed. "That should be made clear at the sale point!"

I wasn't serious, or rather, it wasn't the truth. We'd never had the network go down like that before. Mobile data, sure, along with cell reception. But the Gold Dust Wi-Fi network kept its signal throughout the journey, albeit very weakly in some spots. After all, the company had to sell movie to stream during the trip. Anything to keep those profits up

"Well, that's stupid," the woman said, flopping back against her chair with what looked suspiciously like a sulk. I couldn't believe these people! With everything that was going on, they were worried about watching a movie!

"Listen!" I called, holding my hand in the air to get everyone's attention. The shouts petered out into curious murmurs before stopping altogether, all eyes turned on me. "I cannot express enough how sorry we are for all these inconveniences, but I can assure you all that we are working very hard on getting everything back as soon as possible."

"But—"

"But nothing!" I said, raising my voice a little louder, though refraining from all-out shouting. "I appreciate we've faced some difficulties on this journey, but the best thing we can do is keep calm and keep moving. We'll be stationed in just over thirty minutes."

"And we'll be properly recompensed?"

I sighed and turned to the voice. "Of course," I replied, nodding so deeply it almost became a bow. "Now, if you don't mind, we need to get on."

I put my head down and marched up the rest of the aisle, ignoring any further questions. I grasped Vanessa's arm as I went and pushed her through the door. People were staring, calling out, but I didn't dare make eye contact for fear I would be dragged back into it all. Of all the things that had happened that day, losing Wi-Fi and even losing the lights were nothing. We had to focus on Walter and whoever had committed this crime.

"Nicely done," Vanessa muttered. "I didn't think I'd ever get them to shut up."

I sighed. "They're just scared. I don't blame them."

As soon as we were in the second carriage and the door closed behind us, I spotted Lucas up ahead. He was making the rounds too, trying to keep everyone calm and answer all their queries. I stopped in my tracks and watched. I had to admit I was impressed, not only that he was out here, doing his job, but that he seemed to be handling it very well indeed. This was the best performance I'd seen from him all day. There was potential there, I could see that now. Perhaps Greg was right to hire him after all.

He'd even somehow got Beverly Lyonel on side, and I was surprised to see her smiling up at him like he was her blue-eyed baby or something. I almost laughed at the madness of it all. At least now I knew who we could all call on when we had an awkward customer.

"This isn't a murder mystery game, is it?"

I jumped at the sound of Mr. Wallis's voice, then closed my eyes, wishing the ground would open up and swallow me. Letting them believe that had to have been the most idiotic thing I'd done that day, possibly that month.

"Murder mystery?" Vanessa asked over my shoulder. I could sense her amusement already. She'd have a good laugh about this when I explained it to her.

"I mean, all these people . . . they're worried," he said. "They wouldn't be worried if it was all an act, would they?"

I finally opened my eyes and forced myself to meet his gaze. "No," I said with a wince. "I'm sorry. I was trying to—"

"It's quite all right," Mrs. Wallis replied. She held onto her husband's hand as she smiled at me. "We understand. It must be difficult to keep this many people at ease."

"Thank you," I said. "But I still should have told you the truth in the first place. I don't really know why I didn't."

"It doesn't matter," Mr. Wallis said. "We enjoyed the thought while it lasted. And it's not like anyone has died, is it?"

He laughed and I pursed my lips, glancing quickly at Vanessa.

"Well, er . . ."

"How is Mr. Kendrick?" Mrs. Wallis asked. "He's all right, isn't he?"

I smiled at her, silently grateful that she'd interrupted what was to be my second lie to her in one day. "Yes, thank you. He's doing well. There's no need to worry at all. Now, if you'll excuse me."

"Of course," Mrs. Wallis said. "I have no doubt you are all very busy, what with all these goings-on."

I nodded my thanks, then reached behind me for Vanessa's arm and stormed, once again, up the length of the train, dragging my best friend stumbling behind me.

CHAPTER 16

"Hey," Penny said as I pushed through the kitchen door. "The lights have gone out."

"You're a perceptive one, aren't you?" Vanessa teased. "What gave it away?"

"Don't be mean, Ness," I said, still pulling her through the room with me.

I fell heavily onto one of the stools and immediately slumped, my spine curved and my shoulders hunched as I deflated.

"What happened?" Amy asked, half an eye on us as she examined the dishes coming out of the washer in case they weren't fully clean. That was something I insisted on—better to put them away spotless than risk not noticing a mark when sending them out.

"The lights went out," I replied with simple sincerity. I didn't really know what else to say.

"Right," she said. "Not the best time to ask, I guess."

"No." I sighed, shaking my head. "Sorry, Amy, I didn't mean to snap. Truth is, I have no idea what's going on, and neither, it seems, do the engineers. Only that something isn't right."

"Quite understandable," she said, still focusing on the dishes, but I knew she meant what she said. Amy was good at reading a situation and knowing how to react. "I'm sure it'll all get sorted soon enough."

"What's wrong, Jessica?" Vanessa asked.

She hadn't taken the stool next to me, instead remaining standing, but she rubbed a hand against my back in an attempt at being comforting. I suppose it was comforting in a way, but comfort was the last thing on my mind. I scoffed so loudly that she whipped her hand away and stared at me as though I'd sworn at her.

"What?" she asked again.

"Why does everyone keep asking me that ridiculous question?" I snapped, because it really was a ridiculous question, given the situation we were in.

"I mean . . . apart from the obvious," she said with a little nonchalant shrug. I loved that woman to the ends of the earth, but goodness, she could be annoying sometimes.

"I can't believe how many times I've had to say this, but listen again," I said carefully, making a point. "A man has been murdered and another has been poisoned. Greg's in the infirmary and is acting suspiciously. The train is being run by a spotty teenager who seems to pick and choose when he knows what he's doing. The meal didn't go at all according to plan, and though most seemed to enjoy it, we have had complaints, and you know how much I hate getting complaints."

"I said apart from—"

"Oh, yes, I forgot to add that the train keeps lurching, the power has gone down, and there's a murderer on the loose. That's enough to test anyone's patience, don't you think?"

"Yeah," she said. "But, I mean, apart from all that. What's wrong, Jessica?"

I looked at her in astonishment, my mouth hanging open and with no clue what to say until I saw her lips twitch into a mischievous grin. I let out a single bark of laughter, then another and another, and soon the two of us were laughing uncontrollably, all the tension and stress of the day snapping inside me. It was like a dam had broken, and everything flowed out in the form of laughter.

"Er . . . are you guys all right?" Penny asked.

She held the antibacterial spray in midair, her cloth midwipe across the counter, and for some crazy, irrational reason, that made me laugh even more. That, along with her confusion expression.

"Oh, oh," Vanessa cried, putting a hand on my shoulder and trying to breathe through her giggles. "Oh, it's too much."

"Okay, stop now," I said, as much to myself as to her. "Okay, stop laughing."

I swallowed and took a deep breath, blowing it out of my pursed lips, and finally, my laughter died to a gentle chuckle. I wiped at my eyes and looked up at Vanessa—though I quickly looked away for fear we'd break into giggles again. Amy and Penny were staring at us in absolute horror, and I couldn't blame them. Nothing about this situation was funny, but I think I might have cried if I didn't laugh. This whole day, this whole situation . . . something had to give.

"Sorry," I said. "Sorry. That was very . . . disrespectful of us."

"Sometimes laughter's all you've got," Vanessa said, shrugging. "And if it helps you get through something, then hey, that's what you need to do."

As my breathing returned to normal, I looked at her fully and smiled. She always said the right thing.

"I am continually impressed by your ability to take things in stride, Ness," I said. "It's like nothing affects you at all."

Her smile slipped then, and she sat down slowly, not making eye contact.

"I wouldn't go that far," she said, her voice tinged with sadness. "You've seen me in my own life. Feels like everything's going wrong there too. I s'pose this makes a refreshing change, as weird as that sounds."

"Yeah," I said, taking her hand and clutching it in mine. I knew how stressed she'd been lately. As crazy as it seemed, this probably did feel like a break to her. Focusing on other people's problems always seemed to do that. "We'll get there, though."

"Thanks."

I snorted with laughter as a thought popped into my head. "Hey, I bet you never thought you'd be so stressed you'd want to get caught up in a murder investigation!"

"Honestly, Jessica?" she said. "I never thought I'd get caught up in a murder investigation, period."

"Me neither," Amy said.

"Nor me," added Penny.

"Huh. It's funny the things life throws at us, isn't it?"

Just then, the lights flickered on briefly, and even from this distance we could hear the cheers of the passengers. But then they went out again, and the cheers turned to groans.

"Looks like they're at least on their way to fixing things," Amy said, offering us a weak smile.

"The power issue, at least," I said.

Despite our raucous laughter of moments ago, I felt awful.

We were no one near to solving this mystery and it seemed like, things were getting more dire by the minute. We had a list of suspects as long as my arm and no real answers. We were no closer to catching the killer or even knowing why they did it.

Our investigation had led us exactly nowhere.

We weren't getting justice for Walter; we were just playing games and making a mess of everything.

Our saving grace was that we'd managed to call through to the authorities. They would definitely be waiting for us when we stopped, no thanks to Lucas. They'd sort out this sorry mess.

"Hey," Vanessa said gently. She put a hand to my face and forced me to look at her. "Hey, Jessica. Chin up, yeah? We've done our best."

I smiled at her, then rested my head on her shoulder as she pulled me into a hug. I've never really believed in fate, but it sure did feel like some unknowable force had put Vanessa on the train that day, of all days. Before that morning, I had never even thought of inviting her along, and I don't think she would have thought of it either.

"We've failed, haven't we?" I said, my head still on her shoulder as I stared out the window, unseeing.

"Not until it's over," she said. "And it's not over yet."

I scoffed, though not with malice. "What else can we do?" I asked. "We've questioned everyone and come up with precisely nothing."

"We've still got . . . what? Twenty-five minutes to go?" she said. I sat up and looked at her curiously.

"Yeah, something like that."

"So twenty-five more minutes to come up with a theory, at least. Something to tell the cops, at least."

I made a noncommittal noise. She was right, but I wasn't sure I had the energy anymore. That was when the lights came back on—and stayed on.

"Hallelujah," Vanessa said, throwing her arms up to the heavens.

I smiled. It felt like a sign that finally, things were looking up, that whatever came next would be a resolution of sorts. I knew it wouldn't be as simple as that, but that thought and Vanessa's pep talk buoyed me and pushed me to keep going. My mind kicked into action again, my thoughts whirring wildly. Vanessa was right; we couldn't give up. Not yet. I couldn't allow my self-pity to get in the way of us finding out the truth. And now we had light too!

"You know what still gets me?" I said. "How has someone done all this—got into the motorcar, killed Walter, got back out, hidden away the whole trip, slipped something into Greg's drink, and continued to act normal—without anyone seeing a single thing?"

"There's some impressive stealth there," Vanessa agreed with a nod. "Almost like they're invisible."

"Almost like a cat," Amy mused.

"Or a thief," Penny said with a laugh.

A thief? That set my mind off again. When else had we seen someone sneak in and out without being noticed? A thief . . .

"Oh, my . . ." I began, my mouth open and my brow creased as I put it all together. Yes, this was the piece of the puzzle I'd been missing. It was all starting to make sense.

"What is it?" Vanessa asked.

I turned to her and laughed. "The heist . . . Could this all be connected? It's got to be."

"What are you talking about, lady?" Vanessa asked, looking at me like I was crazy—and not for the first time that day. But I'd make her listen.

"What were you saying about the heist earlier?"

"That the thief used a grapple hook?" Vanessa ventured. "I still think that's true, you know."

"No, no." I shook my head. "You were saying how impressive it was that the guy, the thief, got in and out without anyone seeing a thing."

"Well, yeah, but—" Vanessa said.

"And what did we *just* say about the murderer in this case?"

Vanessa's face tightened and she rubbed at her earlobe as she looked doubtfully at me. "I dunno, Jessica. I don't think—"

"I'm serious!" I cried, leaping to my feet. A thrill of excitement rocketed through me, and yes, I had to admit, it was the same thrill I felt when I worked out some complicated puzzle. Only it was much, much better. "They're connected," I said again. "They've got to be."

Vanessa raised an eyebrow at me. "And you said my theories were far-fetched."

"Well, maybe I was wrong," I said. "Maybe your theories weren't so crazy after all. And this makes perfect sense. Nothing ever happens in Golden, and now we've had a heist and a murder in a matter of days? There's no way that could be a coincidence. Even their MOs are the same. They've got to be connected!"

"I'm not sure stealth counts as an MO," Vanessa snorted. "Isn't that a standard character trait in all criminals? Or all successful ones, at any rate. If your entire theory is based on the fact that both were stealthy and secretive, I really don't think it's strong enough."

"I'm sorry, Jessica," Amy said. "But I agree with Vanessa."

"Me too," Penny said. "I mean, why would the guy who stole the golden spike have a beef with Walter or Greg? It doesn't make sense."

"Unless *they* had something to do with the heist themselves," Amy chuckled.

"Ha!" Vanessa cried. "Can you imagine *Greg* sneaking in anywhere?"

"And what would they want with the spike anyway?" Amy asked.

"You know what Greg's like. Maybe he wanted to use it somewhere on our train. You know, to increase profits."

Penny sniggered at her own joke, and the others followed suit, but I wasn't really listening. Their words swam in the air around me, and while I caught one here and there, they were far from my focus.

They could mock me all they liked, but this idea was screaming at me, flashing right before my eyes.

It felt right—true, somehow.

What had Vanessa said about trusting my instinct? Well, my

instinct was telling me the heist and the murder were somehow connected.

My eyes darted across the floor as the pieces fell into place, one after another, sliding together to make one whole picture. Snippets of conversations I'd heard, sly glances I'd seen, things Greg had said to me . . .

I gasped. "That's it!"

And before anyone could say another word, I ran from the kitchen.

CHAPTER 17

"Greg!" I cried, skidding through the corridor. I grabbed hold of the corner wall and swung around, slamming my hand down on the handle and bursting into the infirmary. "Greg!"

"Whoa there," he said, wide-eyed with amusement. "I know you're keen to see me, but—"

"That night . . . You said you were there!"

"What are you talking about—"

"Thanks for waiting for me!" Vanessa cried as she rounded the corner. She leant heavily on the doorframe, catching her breath. I glanced at her, but I had no time for her right now. I had to get back to Greg, to hear what he had to say.

He was the only one who could prove my theory right, and now I knew how. I also suspected the motive behind Greg's poisoning.

"Well?" I demanded.

He blinked at me, looking so blank and confused I would have laughed if all this wasn't so important. I huffed, closed my eyes briefly, and started again, slower this time. My mother always told me *less haste, more speed*, and if ever there was a situation that applied to, it was now.

"The night of the museum heist—" I began.

"What's the heist got to do with anything?" he asked.

I stopped myself from glaring at his interruption and started again.

"The night of the heist," I repeated. "You said you were in town, right?"

"Right," he said, completely mystified by my line of questioning. His brows were so creased they may have ended up in his eyes if he wasn't careful.

"You walked by the museum, but you saw absolutely nothing of note."

"I was there," he said with a nod. "Like I told you yesterday when we were talking about it, I wish I'd seen something that could help, but I didn't. It was just an ordinary night, nothing special at all."

"What were you doing?" I asked.

"Just . . . I dunno." He shrugged and stuck his bottom lip out. "I went out for a walk. I couldn't sleep, so I thought a wander round town might help. Fresh air always seems to do me good."

"Did it?" Vanessa asked. "Help you sleep?"

I shot her a look, shaking my head at her question. "What does it matter? There are more important things to discuss than insomnia cures right now!"

She smiled awkwardly, then cleared her throat, looking down at the floor. "Never mind. Ignore me."

I turned back to Greg. "Think back. Maybe you did see something."

His frown deepened, and he closed his eyes. I imagined him walking through the town on that warm night again in his mind, the stars above him. I could picture him passing the museum, the theatre, the little row of shops, in a world of his own. He shook his head slowly.

"Think," I urged. "What were the streets like?"

He huffed and tilted his head, but he was still thinking. "The . . . the streets were quiet, I suppose," he said, his face still screwed up with the memory. "I walked past the museum and . . . I don't know; it was the middle of the night." He opened his eyes and looked apologetically at me. "No, there's nothing, Jess. What are you trying to get at?"

I wanted to scream in frustration. I was so sure I was right, but I didn't want to say it and put the idea into his head. I'd read about false memories; I knew it could happen. He had to come to this on his own or not at all. He remembered something, I knew he did—he said as much earlier on. He just had to find that thread and pull on it.

"Try again," I insisted.

"I don't know, Jessica, this is all a bit—"

"Think!" I growled, not wanting him to give up.

Come on, Greg. Come on. You can do it.

"Hey, Jessica," Vanessa said.

I waved my hand behind me, silently begging her to be quiet. Greg sighed and closed his eyes, once again thinking through the events of that night.

"I left my house. It was warm, so I didn't bother with a jacket. I . . . took a left turn down past the museum. There wasn't really anyone about and it was nice. Except . . ."

It felt like an age before it happened, and my heartbeat was so loud it felt like the whole room was thudding in time with me. I couldn't remember the last time I'd been so tense; my whole body was like rock.

And then it came.

Greg gasped and his eyes shot open, a finger raising in the vague direction of the door. "That woman . . ."

"Yes?" I urged. "What about her?"

"That's . . . that's where I know her from. She was there the night of the heist!"

"It's her!" I cried, jumping up with glee. "It's got to be!"

"Wait a minute," Vanessa said. "Will someone please explain to me what's going on."

"That's the connection," I said, more calmly now. "Between the situation here and the heist. That Dani woman, the one with the attitude, she was present at both."

Vanessa shrugged. "That proves nothing. What exactly did you see, Greg?"

I saw him visibly deflate at Vanessa's words.

"She's right, Jessica. All I saw was her walking by the museum. If that makes her a suspect, I must be one too."

"So she was in town and then got on a train," Vanessa continued.

"Maybe she's visiting an aunt or something and wanted to see the sights. It doesn't mean she has anything to do with either, does it?"

"Well, no," I admitted, shifting my weight from foot to foot. "But you've got to agree that it's a pretty big coincidence."

"Coincidence, maybe," Vanessa said. "But Golden's not a very big town. Those sorts of coincidences must happen all the time."

"But it's not like she's even been enjoying the trip," I said quickly with exasperation. "In fact, I'd say she looked like she was positively bored for most of it, if not irritated by it. *And* she was overly interested in Greg's health after he was poisoned. I mean, no one else came to the kitchen to ask after him, did they?"

"That doesn't prove anything either," Vanessa said. "She could have spotted him in town and taken a fancy to him, got herself a crush, asked around, found out he worked on the train, got herself a ticket in the hopes of winning him over."

Greg winked, cocksure. "And who could blame her? Any woman would be lucky to have a piece of me."

I rolled my eyes at him. Even sick and with a murderer on the loose, he could be so arrogant.

"And what about Walter?" Vanessa continued, clearly on a roll.

Ah yes, Walter. That was the only bit that didn't fit.

"Ugh!" I perched on the edge of Greg's bed and blew the air out of my cheeks. "Every time we hit on a theory, there's always something that makes it fall down."

"Sorry, Jessica," Vanessa said with an apologetic shrug, like it was her fault. I was so excited about all this fitting together that I clean forgot about the thing that brought it all together in the first place. Walter was murdered. I wanted to kick myself.

"No, no," Greg said slowly, his finger in the air yet again. "Wait a minute. Let's just think about this. There might be a reason."

"Like what?" I asked, feeling the hope starting to bubble again.

"Earlier, when I was—"

"What the—?" The lights went out again, plunging us into a semi, dusky darkness once more.

"Not again," Vanessa muttered.

"This train never has problems," Greg said, getting up from the bed. "What's going on today?"

As if in answer to his question, the train slowed until it had stopped completely. Somebody didn't want us getting off this train, and I thought I knew why. With Greg alive, the murderer still had work to do, and we were far too close to the end of the line.

"I think someone's messing with us," I said darkly. "Playing a game of cat and mouse. Teasing us."

"Really? I'd hardly call switching the lights on and off the act of a master criminal." Vanessa looked unconvinced, but I didn't have time to explain it to her again. I just knew, in my gut, that I was right.

"Ness, go into the passenger cars and see if you can find Dani. Keep her there."

"Me?" she screeched. "What am I meant to do? Hold her down?"

"Of course not!" I said. "Just keep her occupied. Talk to her. Make some mindless chatter. You're good at that."

Vanessa looked affronted. "Geez, thanks!"

Greg chuckled and I swatted his arm.

"And what if she is the killer?" Vanessa asked, her voice quick and urgent.

"What happened to the brave woman who sneaked a peek at a dead body this morning?" I asked. "Besides, she's got no reason to kill you, and she certainly won't try anything in the middle of a carriage full of people, will she?"

"And what if she's not there?" she asked.

"Then keep looking. She has to be on this train somewhere, and if I am as wrong about all this as you seem to think, then she'll be in her seat, doing nothing wrong, won't she?"

Vanessa looked uncertain, clinging to my gaze for a long moment. I looked back at her, my eyes telling her everything would be all right. Eventually, she nodded.

"Good," I said. "I'm going back to the motorcar to find out what I can. We need to get this train moving again."

"What about me?" Greg asked.

"Stay here!" I snapped, my hair swinging around as I turned back to him. "How many times do I have to tell you that you need to rest?"

"Okay, okay," he said, his hands in the air. "Jeez, Jessica, point taken."

"Thank you," I said, feeling a little embarrassed by my outburst even though I knew I shouldn't—I was perfectly right. Greg still looked pale and his movements were slow, weak.

I threw him a final glance then made my way to the motorcar. The noise had died to a gentle thrumming, though the heat was still almost overwhelming. Up ahead, I could hear voices shouting at one another as they tried to get the train moving again, but their words were muffled and unclear. Ralph was at the switchboard again.

"Any news?" I asked.

"Er . . . no," he said, once more scratching his head and staring at the switches.

"What's the problem, Ralph?" I asked. "Is there some sort of fault?"

"I . . . er." He laughed, but it lacked humor. "You know what, Jessica? I don't know what the problem is. In fact, it seems to me there's no fault at all."

"What do you mean?" I asked, confused by his words.

"It's like . . . hmmm . . ." He turned and looked at me with a shrug. "It looks to me like someone's manually switching it off, but that's crazy, right? Because there's been no one in here and—"

"You mean you haven't *seen* anyone in here."

"Hey, you know what, Jessica?" he said, looking as exhausted as I felt. "We're in and out of here all day long. If someone was coming in, we'd notice, I'm sure of it."

"Not if they were stealthy as a cat," I muttered under my breath.

"What was that?"

"I don't know, Ralph. You said it yourself earlier—it's like something goes wrong every time your back is turned."

"Well, yeah, I did, but that's just one of those things you say, isn't it?"

I shook my head, looking at him seriously. "There's something going on here, Ralph. And I think I know who's behind it."

"Who?" he asked, his interest clearly piqued. "Is it the same person who . . ." He glanced over at the body in the corner.

"You'll find out soon enough," I said, making my way back to the door.

I tried—really, really tried—not to look over at Walter before I left the room. But as I put my hand on the door handle, some unseen force within me made me look back over my shoulder. I took in a deep breath, allowing myself to feel the moment.

"I'll make this right, Walter," I said under my breath. "As right as I can. I promise."

Dani was behind this; she had to be.

She was stealthy enough, sly almost; we knew that already. She could easily have gotten into the motorcar and out again without anyone seeing her. If I was right, she'd stolen the golden spike, for goodness sake!

She was playing with us so that she could finish the job she'd started. She was going to kill Greg.

Greg!

His name came to me on a gasp, and I dashed out of the door, skirting around the office and facilities until I got to the infirmary, where the door was closed.

Closed? Why is it closed? I had left it open, I was sure I had.

I paused for barely a second before bursting through. That's when I saw the glint of the knife.

CHAPTER 18

"Help!"

It was Greg. He cowered on the floor, backed up into a corner, his arm raised over his face. And above him, Dani towered, a chef's knife raised in her left hand. My knife! Of all the things she'd done, she'd had the audacity to go into *my* kitchen and—

"Help!" Greg's scream shook me back to the present, and I drew in a breath. She was going to kill him!

It felt like time slowed. My mouth dry, I froze to the spot, the same words running around and around in my head: *stop her, stop her, stop her.*

Something clattered to the floor as he tried to push himself further back, but to no avail. He was stuck. He couldn't get away from her.

"Stop!" I roared, my voice filling the little room.

Dani glanced over her shoulder at me, her eyes wild with rage. Greg threw his arm up, knocking hers to the side with such force that the knife lodged itself into the wall cladding, and he rolled from under her.

She growled angrily and, with a grunt, yanked the knife out of the wall. She spun around to face Greg. He'd leapt to his feet and stood unsteadily in front of me.

She swiped through the air, missing him by millimeters, but it was enough for him to lose his footing. He swayed, the effects of the poisoning still rushing through him, and staggered toward the bed.

"Greg!"

I called out, but it was too late.

Dani saw his weakness and grabbed hold of him, throwing him easily down onto the bed. She was surprisingly strong for such a small thing, and I faltered, wanting to pull her off him but not sure I could.

Stop her, stop her!

Greg was flat on his back now, and Dani climbed on top of him, straddling him like a lover. She pinned his shoulder down with her right arm, putting her weight on it, and she grinned at him before raising the knife in the air, a look of delight across her features. The cat had finally caught her mouse.

"Dani, stop!" I cried.

To my surprise, she paused, as if my words brought her back to herself. She straightened her back, still on top of Greg, and turned to look at me. This was my chance—my only chance—to convince her. I swallowed back my fear and spoke.

"Listen, Dani," I said. She cocked her head like a confused puppy, and though she still didn't climb off Greg, she lowered the knife at least. "It's over," I said. "There's no way out now."

"There's always a way out," she said, her voice low and menacing. It was entirely different from the bright, friendly voice she used earlier. Even her facial features had changed, darkened somehow. It was like she was a completely different person. Vanessa was right; attitude didn't make someone a killer, but it certainly seemed like a precursor to whoever this was in front of me now.

"Not this time," I said, taking a tentative step forward. I tried to keep my voice calm, sweet even. I wanted her to believe I was on her side. "We know everything. About the heist, about Walter, about Greg. We know it's you who's been messing with the power too."

"And?" She barked with laughter. "What you know won't mean a bean when you're dead."

I shook my head, taking another step closer. "You can't kill us all, Dani," I said. "There are well over a hundred people on this train. *Innocent* people."

"I don't need to kill everyone," she snarled. "Just you and him."

She nodded her head in Greg's direction, and I glanced at him. He shook with terror, his face as white as alabaster, and I knew it was up to me to get us out of this.

"We've called the authorities, Dani. They're meeting us at the station. There's nowhere for you to go. Even if you did kill us, we've got you trapped. Things will only be worse for you if you kill us too. It's too late."

"It's never too late!" she roared and, at the same time, leapt from the bed until she was crouched on the floor in front of me. I threw my hands in the air, my heart racing as she grinned at me. "Not got so much to say now, have you?" she said.

"Dani, wait," I said, my voice urgent, my thoughts muddled.

This is it. This is how I die.

Stop her.

"Say goodbye to the world, Jessica."

"Not on my watch," Greg said, and with an almighty grunt, he struck her over the head.

I whimpered as I watched her go down, just as Vanessa rushed into the room, barging past me and leaping onto Dani's body.

"Got her," she said. "Fetch some rope or something."

"Er . . ."

"I'll go," Greg said, pushing past me and rushing out to the motorcar.

I was grateful. I'm not sure I could have moved even if I wanted to. Adrenaline coursed through my system as I stared down at my best friend lying on top of a murderer to keep her down. Dani squirmed under Vanessa's weight, groaning.

"How did you know?" I asked Vanessa. I think she tried to shrug, but it was difficult to tell when she was so tangled with Dani on the floor.

"I couldn't find her," she said. "Figured she must be at this end of the train, and when I got here, I could hear the things you were saying to her. So I guess I just waited for my moment."

"Thank you," I said—and I meant it. Between her and Greg, they'd saved my life.

"No," she said, shaking her head. "Thank you. You were the one who worked it all out."

"Here," Greg said as he rushed back in, carrying a twist of heavy rope in his hands. "It's amazing what you can find in an engine room."

Together, the three of us managed to tie Dani's hands behind her back, then bound her ankles as well—we weren't taking any chances. We propped her up against the wall, the same corner into which she had pushed Greg earlier, and she sat there, snarling and sulking in equal measure.

"What did you hit her with, anyway?" I asked once she was secured. She didn't seem to have any injury to her head or neck, and she certainly hadn't been cut. There was no blood. She didn't even seem dazed.

Greg looked embarrassed. "It was the first thing I could find," he said.

"What was?" I asked, frowning at him.

That's when he held it up—a thick roll of bandages! I laughed loudly. "Really? After the pillow, quite possibly the softest thing in here!"

"Worked, didn't it?" he said, his lips twisting into a smile.

"Yeah," I said, looking into his eyes and smiling. "It worked. And you managed to disarm her without injuring her. That's got to be worth something."

"As much as I hate to interrupt you both," Vanessa said, winking at me, "how far from the station are we?" She sat on the bed and ran a hand over her face. Greg dropped down next to her. He looked lost, exhausted.

"About fifteen minutes," I said. "Once the train gets moving again."

"I'm sure they're working on it," Greg said.

"What's taking so long?" Vanessa asked.

"It's not easy to get such a hunk of metal moving again," Greg explained. "Especially when the workings are a hundred years old."

"You're all assuming we get to the station at all," Dani snarled.

"We will," Greg reassured her. "Don't you worry about that."

"Why wouldn't we?" Vanessa asked. "Got something else planned?" She looked at each of us in turn, a pout on her lips, but from her expression I could tell there weren't any other tricks to come. She'd tried and she'd failed. She could try and talk her way out of it, but that wouldn't get her anywhere.

I laughed. "Don't you think it's about time you admitted defeat?"

"Never," she said, and she spat on the ground.

"Oh, Dani." I sighed, and though Vanessa patted the bed next to her, inviting me to sit down, I chose to sit on the floor instead, cross-legged and facing the killer we'd hunted down. I wanted to be eye level with her.

I wanted answers.

I looked directly into her eyes and held her gaze for as long as she could stand it. I had so many questions for her. I was so curious. Why would anyone want to do the things she had done today? Or the other day at the museum for that matter.

"So, I get why you wanted to kill Greg," I said. "And I'm guessing the whole heist thing was to do with money. But why Walter? What did he ever do to you?"

Dani sucked her teeth and turned her head away from me, refusing to answer.

"Yeah," Greg said. "What exactly was your problem with Walter?"

"And what about that gold spike?" Vanessa asked. Typical Vanesa to be stuck on the heist. It had been in her head since the moment she heard about it. "Did you work alone? Did you use a grapple hook?"

"A grapple hook?" Dani frowned at Vanessa, clearly as confused as everyone else when it came to the grapple hook.

"Yeah, you know, like in *Batman*," Vanessa said a little sheepishly. Dani merely shook her head and turned away.

"Walter was an innocent man," I said, still looking at her, willing her to turn and talk to me. "He didn't do anything wrong. He had no information about you or know anything he could use against you. You just killed him in cold blood, for no reason."

"He got in the way," she said, her lips pursed.

"How?" I asked. She made no reply, so I repeated my question more forcefully. "How, Dani? How did that poor, innocent man get in your way? What did he do that was so bad you had to take his life from him?"

She huffed. "You really want to know?" she asked, eyebrows raised.

"Of course I do," I snapped. She licked her lips as she looked at me, smirking, and part of me wanted to reach over and throttle her. But I was a better person than she would ever be. I straightened my back and took in a deep breath. "Well?" I asked.

"He was in the wrong place at the wrong time," she said. "I followed that one"—she nodded at Greg—"into the motorcar, but somehow he slipped away without me noticing. Quite impressive, that," she said.

"Impressive?" Greg asked.

"Not many people get away from me, and you've survived three times now." She looked disgusted with herself, like she'd failed. I supposed, in a way, she had.

"And Walter?" I asked, not wanting her to think I'd forgotten. I wouldn't let it drop until I knew her motive. "What about him?"

Dani tutted. "He sneaked up on me, which is rather ironic, really, given it's normally me who does the sneaking. Tapped me on the shoulder and asked me in that stupid voice of his what I was doing in the motorcar."

"So, what?" Vanessa asked. "You just . . . killed him? Just like that? Because you were in a private area and he wanted to know why?"

Dani looked at Vanessa disdainfully, as though she was the worst person in the world. "Obviously not," she said. "I'm neither that impulsive nor that stupid."

"So what happened?" I asked, keeping my anger under wraps. She shrugged, then shifted position as best she could.

"I put on my sweetest voice and told him I was lost. Looking for the facilities. He believed me at first, the idiot." She sniggered. "Started to offer me directions. But then he noticed the flick knife in my hand."

"So you stabbed him?" I asked incredulously

"Of course," she said as though it was nothing. As though she was talking about a film she'd seen or a conversation she'd had.

"What happened to your knife?" I asked. "Because that's one of mine."

"I threw it out of the window when we were going over a trestle bridge. It was covered in blood. What was I meant to do with it?"

"But . . . I don't understand," Greg said. "If you were planning on stabbing me in the first place, why did you end up poisoning me?"

She shrugged again. "Got to have a backup plan," she said. "And I was right, wasn't I? Plan A didn't work, so plan B came into play."

I was astonished by the offhand, dispassionate way she spoke. She really didn't care. What did it take for a person to get like that?

"What about the heist?" Vanessa asked.

Dani sighed. "Almost the greatest success of my career. And no," she spat, looking in my direction, "it was nothing to do with money."

"Then what was it?" Greg asked.

"The challenge, I suppose. It's not the first museum I've hit, but that spike is the biggest loot I've come away with."

"Except you haven't, have you?" I said, perhaps a little maliciously. "Because you failed, and the golden spike will be returned."

She sneered at me again. "Only if you can find it."

"Oh, they'll find it, all right," Vanessa said. "Let me guess . . . sock drawer in your hotel?"

Dani frowned at her, shaking her head. "What?"

"Not the sock drawer then. Under the mattress?"

"Shut up," Dani snapped.

Vanessa laughed. She'd obviously got to Dani, and from the pink flush on her cheeks, I'd say Vanessa wasn't far wrong. The golden spike was somewhere in her hotel room.

The train lurched forward, and I put my hand out to steady myself.

"We're moving!" Vanessa said, a laugh on her lips.

"We sure are," Greg said.

I closed my eyes and sighed with relief, but before I could say anything, Lucas came running into the room.

CHAPTER 19

"What's going on?" Lucas asked, hanging onto the doorframe. "What's wrong?"

I twisted around to get a better look at him. His face was red from exertion, and his chest heaved with his breaths. He looked wildly about the room, and I couldn't help but laugh. How far behind us was he?

"What?" he demanded, clearly not having spotted Dani tied up in the corner. "What's going on? Is everyone—"

"It's all right," Greg said, chuckling at the sight of his intern. "It's all sorted." The words didn't seem to calm him, though.

"But . . ." His eyes fell onto Dani, and he took a step back, a bolt of fear flashing through his eyes. "Oh, I see. I . . . Who . . .?"

"Jessica worked it out," Greg said, smiling warmly at me before turning to face Lucas again. "This is Dani. She's our killer."

It really was something how quickly we got used to the idea that a killer was among us. Before this journey, if someone had told me I'd happily sit in a small room with a killer tied up in the corner, I'd have said they were nuts. There's no way I'd be comfortable with that. Now, after only a few hours, we were bandying the words about like they were nothing: *murder, killer, death.* But whether it was the total immersion or the relief that it was finally over, we were all strangely relaxed with the idea.

"Oh, right, I see," Lucas said, looking as though he did not see at all. I figured it would take a little time for him to catch up. We'd lived it; he hadn't.

"Where've you been, anyway?" Vanessa asked. "Aren't you meant to be interim manager? You're supposed to know everything that's happening on your train, and this is old news now."

"Ness," I said, giggling at her attempt to reprimand him. "Don't be so cruel. He's just a kid. And this is hardly standard procedure for Gold Dust Railways, is it?"

"It's a good question though," Greg said. "Where *have* you been?"

"Ugh!" Lucas shook his head, clearly exhausted by whatever had happened in the last half hour or so. "I got collared by Beverly Lyonel. I'm pretty sure she's a lifer now. We'll be seeing her again, for sure."

"Yes, it looked like you'd found her sweet spot when I saw you talking to her earlier," I said.

"She thinks I'm her new best friend," he said, looking only a tiny bit terrified by that prospect. "Once I got her off my back, I had to deal with Carter, and then Dorothy, and then some guy who wanted to know if he could have some more champagne—on the house, of course, given all the interruptions. I told him there was none left and that I could offer him wine instead, but he insisted I was lying. I swear, it's impossible to walk through that train and have it take less than an hour. Everyone wants a piece of you."

That was the most I'd heard Lucas say all day. It was nice to see him coming out of his shell a little, even if he was ranting about our customers.

Greg laughed. "Now there, my boy, is an important lesson you're going to have to learn. There's nothing wrong with making your polite excuses and moving on."

Lucas nodded. "Yeah, I'll definitely have to learn that trick." He looked around the room. "So . . . everyone's all right, then? No more deaths or, you know, murders?" He looked at Dani when he said that last word, and she glared at him.

"We're better than all right," Greg said, getting to his feet. "I feel fit as a fiddle."

"And you're still getting checked out when we stop," I warned him, my eyebrow raised.

"Yes, Mother," he replied, holding a hand out to help me up. I scowled at him but took his proffered hand and got to my feet. I brushed the dust from my jeans then looked pointedly at Vanessa.

"Right, well, I suppose I ought to go and check on my kitchen," I said.

"But what about her?" Vanessa asked, pointing to Dani. "Can't just leave her here on her own. She's got form."

"We could put her in the motorcar with the body," Lucas suggested.

"That's a bit grim," Vanessa replied.

"It's her bed; she can lie in it," Greg said. "It's kind of fitting, isn't it? Murderer made to wait with her victim."

"It's not a bad idea actually," I said.

"Jess—"

"Where else can we put her, Ness? This keeps her out of the way of the other passengers, and the engineers can keep an eye on her."

"It's agreed then," Greg said, and we each in turn nodded. He grinned down at Dani. "We're going for a little walk," he said.

"Great," she muttered.

I crouched down and pulled at the rope around her ankles, then snatched it up off the floor. She snarled at me the whole time. When I was done, I stepped back, and Greg and Lucas grabbed an arm each, yanking her up from the floor. Together, we marched her to the motorcar, all four of us in some weird, macabre convoy.

"What is it now?" Ralph asked as we entered.

"Do me a favor, Ralph?" Greg said. "We're going to leave her here, tied up. Keep an eye on her, will you? Just make sure she doesn't escape."

"So you're the one, are you?" Ralph asked, his voice low and disdainful. He grunted. "Yeah. Dump her in the corner, there."

Greg shoved her toward the corner, then commanded her to sit.

She glared at him but didn't move. "Sit down," he said again, harsher this time, the words coming from between his teeth.

"Guess we'll have to do this the hard way," Vanessa said.

Dani twisted to get a better look as Vanessa skirted around her. I thought she was going to hit the back of her knees or something, sending her flying to the ground, and I was surprised; Vanessa was not normally one for violence. She didn't *hit* the back of Dani's knees, though. She rubbed gently. Dani, in her surprise, didn't think to move away, instead looking over her shoulder with a creased brow, probably as incredulous and unbelieving as the rest of us.

"Gently does it," Vanessa said in a sing-song voice. "That's it. Down you go. Down you go."

And to my amazement, Dani slowly sank to the floor until she sat with her legs tucked beneath her. From the expression on her face, she was equally astonished, and I'd guess partly because she had allowed it to happen.

"Neat trick," Lucas said.

"Just a little thing I learned in the army," Vanessa said with a nonchalant shrug.

"Right. Lucas, you come with me," Greg said. "Got things to do before the train stops."

"Take it easy though, Greg, yeah?" I said as they turned to walk away.

"Really, Jessie," he said, winking at me over his shoulder. "It's so sweet of you to care."

Wow. Nice Greg didn't last long before he turned back into Arrogant Idiot Greg.

"Jessica," I said firmly, just before they disappeared through the door.

"Yeah, yeah," he said, chuckling.

"Hey," I said to Vanessa once they were out of sight. "You were never in the army."

Vanessa threw me a cheeky smile. "No," she said. "But they don't know that."

I laughed. "Come on, you. Let's get back to the kitchen and check on the girls."

142

Pride surged through me as I walked into the passenger carriages , holding my head up liked we'd achieved something wonderful.

We had, of course, but no one really knew yet.

Although there were still the odd grumbles of dissatisfaction, everyone seemed much happier and calmer now, and we even got a few smiles.

Beverly Lyonel looked more relaxed than I'd ever seen her, and I couldn't help but wonder what Lucas had done to achieve that. Mr. and Mrs. Wallis were chatting excitedly to the woman in the seat opposite them. It seemed they were planning on attending a real murder mystery party together. It warmed my heart to see everyone more settled. If we could get them having a good time even with everything that happened today, we were doing our jobs right.

We carried on up the train to where Carter and Dorothy were bickering, as always—some things will never change, and that, too, was nice to see. They were as much a part of this train as Greg or I were now.

"Oh, Jessica, dear," Dorothy said as I approached, her hand in the air to stop me. I looked down at the huge diamond ring that glittered on her leathery soft fingers and smiled. I can't believe I ever doubted old Dorothy, but then, I'd doubted every single person on the train at one point or another.

"Hi again," I said. "I'm sorry about all the interruptions today. I hope it hasn't spoiled your enjoyment too much."

"Nonsense," she said firmly. "This has been the most exciting trip yet! We just never knew what was going to happen next."

I chuckled. "I do hope that won't put you off booking with us again," I said. "I doubt Greg will allow quite so much to go wrong on the next trip."

"Never." She took my hand in hers and patted it. "You're all like family to me now. Even that miserable so-and-so over there."

"Hey, I heard that," Carter said.

"As you were meant to," Dorothy said.

"Of course," I heard Vanessa say to someone. "Yes, we completely understand. Ah, yes. No, no, you'll be reimbursed. Everyone will be reimbursed."

I turned my wide eyes on her. She couldn't be offering everyone refunds, could she? She didn't even work for the railway, and she certainly had no authority to be handing out refunds.

"In fact," she said in one of her loudest voices. "You'll all be getting free tickets too!"

I almost choked on my own breath. Greg was going to kill her.

"Ness! You can't just—"

"Oh, stop fretting," she said, waving her hand in the air dismissively.

"But Greg—"

"Believe me, Greg will be happy when he sees the result. Every single person will go home talking about this trip and feeling good because they got a freebie. And that'll get other people talking too. You just watch ticket sales go up."

I stared at her in astonishment, my mouth hanging open, but then I had to laugh at her audacity and I pulled her into an embrace.

"You're the best, you know that, Ness?"

"Yes, I know," she said, feigning a tired sigh.

I leant into her, nudging her playfully. "Come on. We'll be stopped soon, and I want to check on Penny and Amy."

We took a few more steps before I saw it. There, at the far end of the second coach, was Dani's empty seat. We paused, silently agreeing we needed a moment.

"You did it, Jessica," Vanessa said to me, our arms entwined and our hands clasped together.

"No, Ness," I said, turning to look at her. "*We* did it."

By the time we reached the kitchen, we were falling over ourselves in laughter and merriment.

"Huh," Penny said, looking at us in surprise. "They've finally broken."

"Seems like something's improved in your world," Amy said brightly.

They'd finished with the dishes, and the countertops were all clean. In fact, the kitchen looked spotless. I could always rely on them to do a good job.

"Our Jessica here worked it all out," Vanessa said, cuddling into my arm. "She's a genius!"

"But you should have seen the way the way Vanessa came running in, pouncing on Dani and holding her down," I said.

"It was nothing," Vanessa said with an eye roll. "Although I did feel a bit like a hero, I must admit."

"Dani?" Penny asked. "Should I know that name?"

"Nope," I said. "And good job too. She's not the kind of person you would want to associate with."

"But Lucas on the other hand . . ." Vanessa said, waggling her eyebrows in Penny's direction. Penny's cheeks flushed in an instant.

"What's going on with you two, anyway?" I asked.

"Nothing," Penny insisted. "We're just friends."

"But you want there to be," Vanessa replied. It wasn't a question. "Word of advice. Get in there while he's still so smitten. Men are at their best when they're like that."

"That's true enough," I snorted. "Listen, thank you so much for today, both of you. You've gone above and beyond, especially in such a difficult situation. I really appreciate it."

"Any time," Amy replied.

"Yeah, anything for you," Penny said. "And I've enjoyed having the extra responsibility today. I feel like I learned a lot."

"Good. Now, go on, the pair of you. We're only minutes away from the station. Get yourselves ready to get off."

Once we'd said our goodbyes, Vanessa and I found ourselves alone. I shrugged off my chef's whites and shoved them roughly into my bag, then untied my apron and threw it into the pile of dirty tablecloths and towels ready to be washed.

"Thank you, Ness," I said. "You've been amazing on this trip."

"What else are best friends for?" Vanessa chuckled. "I bet when you suggested me coming for a ride, you weren't expecting it to be this exciting."

"Nope," I admitted. "I thought it would do you good, take your mind off your own stresses, but today has taken it to another level!" I picked my bag up and swung it over my shoulder. "I don't know about you, but I'm exhausted now."

"Got enough energy for a quick drink?" she asked, looking at me with that cheeky grin of hers. "That bar on the corner does a lovely glass of red."

"Sounds good to me," I said, holding open the kitchen door for her. We were just pulling into the station. "But we've got to get through the authorities first and make sure Greg has his checkup as promised!"

"Meh!" Vanessa laughed. "Maybe while we're at it, you can teach them a thing or two about investigating."

I snorted loudly. "Hardly! I'm a chef, remember?"

"And a very good one too," Vanessa said. "But d'you know what? I think maybe you're a bit of a detective, after all."

CHAPTER 20

The train doors hissed open, and I stepped out onto the platform, Vanessa just behind me. The air was filled with the scent of diesel, and the station was bustling with bodies, people dragging luggage or pulling a toddler through a turnstile. I could hear the different trains along each platform, could feel their gentle thrumming in my heart. There was the whistle of the station master and the call of the signalman. I smiled, raising my face up to the early evening sun, and sighed happily. I was always satisfied at the end of a trip, but today it felt extra special.

I looked up the length of the train, watching as the passengers filed off. Despite everything that had happened, every single person who stepped down from the train did so with a smile on their lips or laughter bubbling into the warm air. Dorothy even waggled her fingers in a wave when she spotted me there, watching. We'd succeeded, we'd won, and I couldn't stop smiling about it.

At the very far end of the train, Greg stood on the metal steps, talking to the group of police officers who were on the platform. That brought it all home again, and I felt a pinch of sadness in my chest. Though I would never have called Walter a friend, as such, his loss would play heavily on me for a long time to come, if not for the rest of my life. I was glad that I could do that one thing—catch the culprit—

for him and for his memory. His untimely death would never be made right, but at least now justice could be served.

And, of course, we'd caught the museum heist thief too.

That added bonus felt really good.

Greg stepped aside and let four police officers file onto the train while one—the chief, I presumed—remained on the platform. Greg looked up at me and beckoned for me to join them. I shook my head. I'd done what he'd asked of me. I was ready to go home. But then the officer turned to me, and he beckoned as well.

"Looks like that glass of red is going to have to wait," I muttered to Vanessa over my shoulder.

"You didn't really think you'd be able to slip away without talking to the police first, did you?" she asked as we began to make our way to them.

I shrugged. "Not really, but I was hoping."

"Come on." She nudged me with her shoulder. "I'm sure it won't take ten minutes, then we'll be out of here."

"Ms. Preston," the officer said, offering me his hand. It was warm, and his handshake firm. "I'm Sheriff James Williamson. First of all, may I express my condolences for what happened today."

He was a tall, broad man, and I could see how he cut an intimidating figure when he chose to. His eyes were bright with intelligence, and he had a kind face, one that you couldn't help but want to talk to. But deep inside, there was a sheen of something, some lost hope or perhaps the haunting of all he had seen in his long career. My little taste of investigation was nothing compared to what this man had experienced.

"Thank you, Sheriff," I said. "It all came as quite a shock, I can tell you."

"I can imagine. Mr. Kendrick was telling me that we have you to thank for the identification and capture of the culprit, and that in the process, you discovered the truth about the museum heist."

"It was a team effort," I said, shifting my weight from foot to foot. I couldn't deny I felt uncomfortable. I didn't want to take credit for any of it except for the meal we provided, and even that I couldn't have done without the help of my team.

"Come off it, Jessie," Greg said.

"Jessica."

"We could never have done it without you," he continued, ignoring my correction. "Honestly, Sheriff, she worked it all out."

"We'd like to—"

"Excuse me." I turned to see a paramedic, a small bag in his hand. "We're here for"—he looked down at his piece of paper—"Mr. Kendrick?"

"That would be me," Greg said, hopping down from the train step. "But I'm feeling fine now, so—"

"It's always best to get it checked out," the paramedic said. "You'd be surprised how many injuries and accidents look like they have no consequence, only to cause serious damage later on."

"Now where have I heard that before?" he asked, looking at me with a wink.

I rolled my eyes.

"If you'll come with me, Mr. Kendrick," the paramedic continued. "You can tell me exactly what happened while we take a look at you. The ambulance is just outside the station."

"All right," he said with a sigh. "If it'll make you all feel better."

"Just go, Greg," I said, tired of his backchat and his nonsense.

"As I was saying, Ms. Preston," Sheriff James said, dragging my attention back to him. "We strongly advise against members of the public investigating crimes themselves. It can be very dangerous, and you put yourselves at great risk."

"I . . . I'm sorry, Sheriff. Given the situation, there was little else we could do."

"Yes," he said with a polite nod. "I can see that, and we appreciate you were doing your civic duty. Despite the dangers you put your-selves in, we are grateful for your assistance in this case. Not only have you helped to bring Mr. Mansell's murderer to justice, but you discovered more about the museum heist perpetrator than we had in two days. For that, we must thank you."

Before I could answer, I heard feet clanking on the metal steps of the train. I turned to see Dani being frog-marched, her hands cuffed behind her back. She glared at me as she passed, but I stared confidently back at her.

"Dani Stanton, sir," one of the officers said. "Says she wants to talk to someone higher up, make sure her case is properly heard."

"I'll tell you where the spike is," Dani said. "But I want something in return."

"I would hardly say you are in a position to negotiate, Ms. Stanton," Detective Williamson said. He looked up at the officer holding her arms. "Take her away."

"It's somewhere in her hotel room," I said. "She didn't say that in as many words, but I'm pretty sure if you search the room, you'll find it."

"We'll make sure to do that," he said. "We'll need to take a full statement from you and from Ms.—" He raised his eyebrows at Vanessa.

"Scott," Vanessa said.

"And from Ms. Scott, and I have an officer taking down the details of all the passengers as they leave the platform."

"Now?" I asked, hoping that would not be the case. I wanted nothing more than to relax after a very long day. I let out a sigh of relief when he shook his head.

"No, but within the next forty-eight hours." He reached into his pocket and pulled out a half-crumpled business card. I took it and read his name: *Detective Daniel Williamson*. "Either come down to the station yourselves, or call me and I'll send someone to pick you up."

"Thank you, Sheriff," I said. He nodded, then marched off in pursuit of Dani and his officers.

"He seemed like a nice guy," Vanessa said, watching him go. "And a bit of a looker, too, if you don't mind my saying."

"Really?" I turned my surprised eyes on her.

She shrugged, but with a laugh. "What? No harm in a girl looking, is there?"

"No," I said, taking her arm in mine. "No harm at all. Shall we . . ."

I didn't finish my sentence. I was distracted by the noise. When I turned to look, I quickly lowered my head in a respectful bow. Two officers were carrying a stretcher on which Walter lay, zipped up in a black body bag. When they reached the platform, something on the stretcher released and two sets of wheels dropped from the bottom.

"Goodbye, Walter," I said.

"Hey," Vanessa said softly, a gentle hand against my arm. "You need a minute?"

I turned and looked at her sadly, my lips pressed together. "No," I said, shaking my head. "No, I'm fine. Come on, let's get going."

As we walked into the parking lot, there was the ambulance, Greg perched on the back with a blanket around his shoulders.

"Hey, Ness?" I asked. "Give us a minute, yeah?"

"Oh no," she said, a hand to her chest and a look of horror across her face. "Tell me it's not true, Jessica?"

"What?" I asked with a bubble of laughter.

"You're not . . . you know . . . with him again, are you?" She broke into a giggle as I slapped her arm.

"Give me some credit, will you? I just want to check he's all right. That's all."

"Yeah, yeah. I'll wait in the car."

"Thanks, Ness."

I watched her go, then turned and made my way to the ambulance.

"How are you feeling now?" I asked.

"I told you, Jessica, I'm feeling fine."

"We're taking him overnight," the paramedic said, looking up from his clipboard. "Just in case. We want to run some tests to find out exactly what it was he ingested. But I hear it was your quick thinking that got him back on his feet and possibly saved his life."

I shrugged. "I only did what any first-aider would have done."

"Right," the paramedic said, looking pointedly at Greg. "You've got one minute, then we're leaving. Got it?"

"Got it," he replied.

We looked at each other as we waited for the paramedic to make his way around to the front of the ambulance, then we both spoke at the same time.

"Listen, I—"

"About that—" I laughed. "You go first."

"I know we don't always see eye to eye, Jessica," he said. "And I get that I wind you up a lot. But I just want you to know how grateful I was to have you there today. In fact, I'm grateful to have you there every day. I wasn't lying earlier when I said we couldn't have done it without you. It would have just descended into chaos."

"There's really no need to thank me, Greg. I—"

"No, really," he insisted. "Jessica, you saved my life. That's something only a truly special person would do."

I laughed, throwing my head back. "I appreciate your words, Greg. But don't think that what happened today means we'll be friends after this." I threw him a warning look, though I could feel the corners of my lips turning into a smile. "I'm sure you'll come up with some ridiculous idea for my kitchen that I'll have to implement in no time at all."

"But you did such a good job today," he cried. "You certainly rose to the challenge!"

"You know, I'll put you on the right path sooner or later," I said. "You'll learn that I'm always right."

"No, that can't be true," he said, his brow creased in mock confusion.

"Oh no? Why's that?"

"Because *I'm* always right," he said.

I snorted with laughter. "You wish."

"All right, Mr. Kendrick, time to go."

I smiled and nodded my understanding at the paramedic, then turned back to Greg. "Bye then," I said.

"Bye, Jessica. See you on the next trip."

I watched as the doors were closed on him, then as the ambulance pulled away, the lights flashing but the siren silent. I knew, without a doubt, that Greg would return to being the temperamental train manager he always was. And no, we probably wouldn't become friends, not really. But at least we'd come to some sort of understanding today, and I knew a little better how to handle him in the future.

I jogged back to the cab. Vanessa was in already in the driver's seat, fixing her hair in the rearview mirror. Though our day hadn't turned out anything like we were expecting, it had accomplished what I had hoped for, because sitting in the car alone, Vanessa looked relaxed, and she had a smile on her face.

I opened the door and got in, grinning at her.

"Everything all right?" she asked. She flipped the visor up, turned the key in the ignition, and put the car into gear.

"Yeah," I said. "Everything's all right."

"So," she said as we pulled out of the lot and onto the main road. "What's our next adventure going to be?"

<><><>

THANK YOU FOR READING RUNAWAY MURDER! I HOPE YOU LOVE Jessica and her family (and Golden!) as much as I do. Take a sneak peek at Golden's Restoration! Join Hope as she returns home to Golden in **MURDER AT THE CLOCKTOWER!**

IN THE HISTORIC TOWN OF GOLDEN, NOT EVERYTHING THAT GLITTERS IS . . .

The rising price of gold has brought a whole new boom to the small town of Golden, California, now in desperate need of renovation. The downtown has to be updated, the historic museum rebuilt, and the beloved Golden Miner statue restored.

Hope Wilson is the perfect candidate for updating the dilapidated clock tower, and even though she's a Golden girl at heart, the town holds painful memories for her. Her husband was killed in a tragic kayaking accident, and her grief was so strong she fled town. Now, after circumnavigating the globe, she may be ready to take on this new assignment . . . .if it weren't that her rebuffed, bitter high school sweetheart, Dustin Lyons, is now in charge of funding the restorations.

That. And there's a body in the clock tower.

Can Hope manage to win Dustin over?

First, she'll have to stop the crime spree in town, but she won't get far without Dustin's help. Together they'll have to save the renovation project and stop a cold-hearted killer.

One-click MURDER AT THE CLOCKTOWER

. . .

IF YOU LOVED RUNAWAY MURDER, YOU'LL LOVE THE FAST-PACED fun of **A FIRST DATE WITH DEATH**. Some are in it for love . . . others for the cash. Georgia just wants to stay alive . . .

AND DON'T MISS MY **YAPPY HOUR** SERIES. IT'S SWEET AND FUNNY and you'll laugh out loud as Maggie, not quite a dog lover, hunts down a murderer. Will Maggie's investigation kill her budding romance with Officer Brooks?

AND IF YOU'RE LOOKING FOR SOMETHING MAGICAL, TRY **A WITCH CALLED WANDA**. Will fledging witch Maeve reverse the curse that has Chuck doomed to live the rest of his days as a female dog . . . or will someone get away with murder?

STAY IN TOUCH! VISIT ME AT **WWW.DIANAORGAIN.COM** TO FIND OUT about new releases and for exclusive sneak peeks of future books. I appreciate your help in spreading the word about my books, including telling a friend. Reviews help readers find books! Please leave a review on your favorite book site.

AND NOW . . . FOR A SPECIAL PREVIEW . . . IF YOU HAVE NOT READ MY MATERNAL INSTINCTS MYSTERIES, you're in for a treat. Join millions of readers and find out what all the fuss is about. Turn the page for an excerpt from the first book in the **BUNDLE OF TROUBLE** . . .

CHAPTER ONE OF BUNDLE OF TROUBLE

A MATERNAL INSTINCT MYSTERY

Labor

The phone rang, interrupting the last seconds of the 49ers game.

"Damn," Jim said. "Final play. Who'd be calling now?"

"Don't know," I said from my propped position on the couch.

I was on doctor's orders for bed rest. My pregnancy had progressed with practically no hang-ups, except for the carpal tunnel and swollen feet, until one week before my due date when my blood pressure skyrocketed. Now, I was only allowed to be upright for a few minutes every couple of hours to accommodate the unavoidable mad dash to the bathroom.

"Everyone I know is watching the game. It's gotta be for you," Jim said, stretching his long legs onto the ottoman.

I struggled to lean forward and grab the cordless phone.

"Probably your mom," he continued.

I nodded. Mom was checking in quite often now that the baby was two days overdue. An entire five minutes had passed since our last conversation.

"Hello?"

A husky male voice said, "This is Nick Dowling . . ."

Ugh, a telemarketer.

". . . from the San Francisco medical examiner's office."

I sat to attention. Jim glanced at me, frowning. He mouthed, "Who is it?" from across the room.

"Is this the Connolly residence?"

"Yes," I said.

"Are you a relative of George Connolly?"

"He's my brother-in-law."

"Can you tell me the last time you saw him?"

My breath caught. "The last time we saw George?"

Jim stood at the mention of his brother's name.

"Is he a transient, ma'am?" Dowling asked.

I felt the baby kick.

"Hold on a sec." I held out the phone to Jim. "It's the San Francisco medical examiner. He's asking about George."

Jim froze, let out a slight groan, then crossed to me and took the phone. "This is Jim Connolly."

The baby kicked again. I switched positions. Standing at this point in the pregnancy was uncomfortable, but so was sitting or lying down for that matter. I got up and hobbled over to Jim, put my hands on his back and leaned in as close as my belly would allow, trying to overhear.

Why was the medical examiner calling about George?

"I don't know where George is. I haven't seen him for a few months." Jim listened in silence. After a moment he said, "What was your name again? Uh-huh . . . What number are you at?" He scratched something on a scrap of paper then said, "I'll have to get back to you." He hung up and shoved the paper into his pocket.

"What did he say?" I asked.

Jim hugged me, his six-foot-two frame making me feel momentarily safe. "Nothing, honey."

"What do you mean, nothing?"

"Don't worry about it," he whispered into my hair.

I pulled away from Jim's embrace and looked into his face. "What's going on with George?"

156

Jim shrugged his shoulders, and then turned to stare blankly at the TV. "We lost the game."

"Jim, tell me what the medical examiner said."

He grimaced, pinching the bridge of his nose. "A body was found in the bay. It's badly decomposed and unidentifiable."

Panic rose in my chest. "What does that have to do with George?"

"They found his bags on the pier near where the body was recovered. They went through his stuff and got our number off an old cell phone bill. They want to know if George has any scars or anything on his body so they can . . ." His shoulders slumped. He shook his head and covered his face with his hands.

I waited for him to continue, the gravity of the situation sinking in. I felt a strong tightening in my abdomen. A Braxton Hicks?

Instead of speaking, Jim stood there, staring at our blank living room wall, which I'd been meaning to decorate since we'd moved in three years ago. He clenched his left hand, an expression somewhere between anger and astonishment on his face. He turned and made his way to the kitchen.

I followed. "Does he?"

Jim opened the refrigerator door and fished out a can of beer from the bottom shelf. "Does he what?" He tapped the side of the can, a gesture I had come to recognize as an itch to open it.

"Have any scars or . . ." I couldn't finish the sentence. A strange sensation struck me, as though the baby had flip-flopped. "Uh, Jim, I'm not sure about this, but I may have just had a contraction. A real one."

I cupped my hands around the bottom of my belly. We both stared at it, expecting it to tell us something. Suddenly I felt a little pop from inside. Liquid trickled down my leg.

"I think my water just broke."

<><><>

Jim expertly navigated the San Francisco streets as we made our way to California Pacific Hospital. Even as the contractions grew stronger, I couldn't stop thinking about George.

Jim's parents had died when he was starting college. George, his only brother, had merely been fourteen, still in high school. Their Uncle Roger had taken George in. George had lived rent-free for many years, too many years, never caring to get a job or make a living.

Jim and I often wondered if so much coddling had incapacitated George to the point that he couldn't, or wouldn't, stand on his own two feet. He was thirty-three now and always had an excuse for not holding a job. Apparently, everyone was out to get him, take advantage of him, "screw" him somehow. At least that's the story we'd heard countless times.

The only thing George had going for him was his incredible charm. Although he was a total loser, you'd never know it to talk to him. He could converse with the best of them, disarming everyone with his piercing green eyes.

Uncle Roger had finally evicted George six months ago. There had been an unpleasant incident. Roger had been vague about it, only telling us that the sheriff had to physically remove George from his house. As far as we knew, George had been staying with friends since then.

I glanced at Jim. His face was unreadable, the excitement of the pending birth diluted by the phone call we had received.

I touched Jim's leg. "Just because his bags were found at the pier doesn't mean it's him."

Jim nodded.

"I mean, what did the guy say? The body was badly decomposed, right? How long would bags sit on a pier in San Francisco? Overnight?"

"Hard to say," he muttered.

I rubbed his leg trying to reassure him. "I can't believe any bag would last more than a couple days, max, before a transient, a kid, or someone else would swipe it."

Jim shrugged and looked grim.

A transient? Why had the medical examiner asked that? George had always lived on the fringe, but homeless?

Please God, don't let the baby be born on the same day we get bad news about George.

Bad news—what an understatement. How could this happen? I closed my eyes and said a quick prayer for George, Jim, and our baby.

I dug my to-do list out from the bottom of the hospital bag.

To Do (When Labor Starts):
1. Call Mom.
2. Remember to breathe.
3. Practice yoga.
4. Time contractions.
5. Think happy thoughts.
6. Relax.
7. Call Mom.

OH, SHOOT! I'D FORGOTTEN TO CALL MOM. I FOUND MY CELL PHONE and pressed speed dial. No answer.

Hmmm? Nine P.M., where could she be?

I left a message on her machine and hung up.

I looked over the rest of the list and snorted. What kind of idealist had written this? Think happy thoughts? Remember to breathe?

I took a deep breath. My abdomen tightened, as though a vise were squeezing my belly. Was this only the *beginning* of labor? My jaw clenched as I doubled over. Jim glanced sideways at me.

He reached out for my hand. "Hang in there, honey, we're almost at the hospital."

The vise loosened and I felt almost normal for a moment.

I squeezed Jim's hand. My husband, my best friend, and my rock. I had visualized this moment in my mind over and over. No matter what variation I gave it in my head, never in a million years could I have imagined the medical examiner calling us right before my going into labor and telling us what? That George was dead?

Before I could process the thought, another contraction overtook me, an undulating and rolling tightening, causing me to grip both my belly and Jim's hand.

When my best friend, Paula, had given birth, she was surrounded mostly by women. Me, her mother, her sister, and of course, her husband, David. All the women were supportive and whispered words of encouragement while David huddled in the corner of the room, watching TV. When Paula told him she needed him, he'd put the TV on *mute*.

When I'd recounted the story for Jim, he'd laughed and said, "Oh, honey, David can be kind of a dunce. He doesn't know what to do."

Another vise grip brought me back to the present. Could I do this without drugs? I held my breath. Urgh! *Remember to breathe.*

I crumpled the to-do list in my hand.

Bring on the drugs.

CHAPTER TWO OF BUNDLE OF TROUBLE

A MATERNAL INSTINCT MYSTERY

*a*fter checking into the hospital and spending several hours in "observation," we were finally moved to our own labor and delivery room.

"When can I get the epidural?" I asked the nurse escorting us.

"I'll call the anesthesiologist now," she said, leaving the room.

Jim plopped himself onto the recliner in the corner and picked up the remote control.

"Hey, I'm having contractions here . . . they're starting to get strong. Aren't you supposed to be breathing with me?"

"Right," he nodded, flipping through the channels. "He he he, ha ha ha," he said in an unconvincing rendition of Lamaze breathing.

"Jim!"

"Hmmm?"

"I need your help now."

His eyebrows furrowed. "No TV?"

"Get me the epi . . . oooh."

He pressed the *mute* button. I sighed and gave in to the contractions.

<><><>

Another hour passed before the anesthesiologist walked in. I was horrified to see that he looked all of about seventeen.

"Sorry to make you wait," he said. "There was an emergency C-section."

"I'm just glad you're here now," Jim said.

The anesthesiologist laughed. "How are we doing?"

"She's doing great, really great," Jim said.

I would have told him to shut up, but that would have taken more energy than I had. Was this teeny bopper qualified to put a fifteen-inch needle in my spine? What *exactly* could go wrong with the epidural? I was about to chicken out when the nurse rushed in.

"Oh, here you are," she said to the anesthesiologist. "Let's go, before she's too far along."

Before I could back out, my torso and legs were blissfully numb.

The nurse placed a metal contraption, resembling a suction cup, on my belly and studied a monitor. "Do you feel anything?"

"Nope."

"Good, because that was a big contraction."

I smiled. "I didn't feel a thing."

The anesthesiologist nodded as he left the room. The nurse advised us to get some rest. Jim returned to the recliner and put the volume back up on the TV. I glanced at the clock: 3 A.M. already. Where was my mother?

My thoughts drifted back to George. What had his bags been doing on the pier? An image of a swollen corpse with a John Doe tag on its foot crept into my mind. I shook my head trying to dissociate the image from George and willed myself to think sweet, pink, baby thoughts.

I scratched my thigh to double-check the effectiveness of the epidural.

During my pregnancy, I had heard dozens of horror stories about infants with umbilical cords wrapped around their tiny necks, only to have the doctor push the infant's head back into the birth canal and perform an emergency C-section. In most of the stories the poor mother had to go through the C-section without any anesthesia. At least I'd already had the epidural.

At 7 A.M., the door to the room opened and my mother appeared, dressed in jeans and sneakers, with binoculars around her neck.

"How you doing?" she asked cheerfully. Without waiting for a reply, she reached up and put two hands on Jim's shoulders pulling him down to her five-foot-two level to kiss his cheeks. After which she handed him her purse and said, "I'm here now, Jim. You can sleep."

Jim smiled, clutched the purse, and happily retreated to his cot. Mom had adopted Jim long ago, even before we were married; it was a relationship Jim treasured since he had lost his own parents so many years earlier.

Just seeing Mom relaxed me. She placed her freezing hands on my face and kissed my cheeks. "Are you running a fever?"

"No. Your hands are cold. Where have you been? You look like a tourist," I joked.

"What do you mean?"

I indicated the binoculars.

"Well, I want pictures of my first grandchild!"

From Jim's corner came a snorted laugh, the kind that comes out through your nose when you're trying to suppress it. I laughed freely.

"What?" Mother demanded.

"They're binoculars," Jim said.

Mother glanced down at her chest.

"Oh, dear! I meant to grab the camera."

Jim relaxed, lying back on the cot.

Mom stroked my hair, then leaned over and kissed my forehead.

"You're frowning," she said.

"I'm worried about the baby. I'm worried about George." I looked over at Jim. His eyes filled with tears.

"George?" Mom turned to look at Jim. Jim covered his face with his hands.

Mom clucked. "Let's start with the baby. Why are you worried?"

I shook my head and took a deep breath. "Don't know. Nervous, maybe."

Mom patted my hand. "Well, that's normal. Everything is going to be fine. When did your labor start?"

"Around nine last night. Didn't you get our messages? Jim must have called at least three times. Where were you?"

Mom settled herself in the chair next to my bed. "I was at Sylvia's. She had a dinner party. There was a lady there who wanted to take home some leftover crackers. Can you imagine? They had sat out all night on an hors d'oeuvres plate. And she wanted to take them home!"

Mom knew me too well. She was making small talk, trying to distract me from thinking thoughts full of doom and gloom. It was working. I was actually laughing.

I peered over at Jim. His eyes were closed, a grimace on his face. He wasn't listening to Mom. He was stressed out. Mom followed my gaze.

"Now, what's happened with George?"

Jim flinched. "Let's not go there, Mom. We got a phone call, right, Kate? Just a call—"

I clutched Mom's hand. "Not just a call! It was a call from the medical examiner. They found a body in the bay and George's bags on the pier."

Mom eyes turned into saucers and she gasped.

"We don't really know anything yet," Jim said. "Let's not get all melodramatic."

Mom and I exchanged looks. "Everything will be fine, you'll see." She gave my hand a squeeze, then released it and folded her hands into her lap.

An awkward silence descended over us. Just then the nurse slipped into the room. "Don't mind me," she said. "I want to see how far along we are."

Jim watched the nurse, his brow creased in concern. I tried to remain calm, my attention returning to the beeping monitor reporting the baby's heart rate.

"Oh, goodness, the baby's practically here," the nurse announced.

I sat up a little. Mom clapped her hands in childish delight and Jim crossed the room to stand next to me.

"I'll call your doctor," the nurse said, turning to leave.

Mom started to follow her. "I'll be right back. I just need to feed my parking meter."

The nurse spun around and stared at Mom. "Don't leave now. You may miss the birth."

"The baby's coming that fast?" Mom asked.

"I hope I can get the doctor here in time," the nurse said, rushing out.

"I hope I don't get a ticket," Mom said.

I laughed. "Why didn't you park in the hospital parking lot?"

Mom shrugged. "There was a spot in front." She hurried across the room to the window, straining to get a peek at her car.

Jim tried to hide the smile that played on his lips. He leaned in close to me and whispered, "Here I am worried about you, the baby, and my brother the screw-up, while I could be worrying about really important stuff like getting a parking ticket."

I giggled. "Or who took home stale crackers from a party."

Our eyes locked. Jim's face broke into a huge smile. "I love you, Kate."

Mom came away from the window. "No ticket yet, that I can *see*."

Dr. Greene, my ob-gyn, popped into the room, her brown hair held in place with two tortoiseshell clips. She walked straight to my side, looking confident in her blue scrubs. She smiled into my face. "How are you doing, Kate?"

"Okay, I guess. I don't feel a thing."

She smiled wider. "That's the beauty of modern medicine. Just push when I tell you."

After about twelve minutes of pushing, Dr. Greene said the words I'll never forget in all my life: "Kate, reach down and grab your baby."

What? She wanted me to pull the baby out?

Startled by her words, I instinctively reached down.

There she was. I grasped my baby girl and pulled her to my chest.

I clutched her to me with a desperation I had never felt before, trying to press her right into my heart. Everyone else in the room seemed to fade into the background. My little angel, my little love.

She was the most beautiful thing in the world. Her round, pretty face was punctuated with a button nose, and strawberry blond hair graced the top of her head. Dark blue eyes peered at me, examining me with the wisdom of an old soul.

I realized Jim was crying. He reached down and enveloped the baby and me in his arms and I forgave him for muting the TV.

Out of the corner of my eye, I saw Mom pull a hankie from her purse and wipe a tear. "Don't worry, darling, I've already memorized her face. No one's switching her on us."

TO KEEP READING...

MATERNAL INSTINCTS

*B*ook 1 from Maternal Instincts Available at no cost...

Click here to get your copy now.

GET SELECT DIANA ORGAIN TITLES FOR FREE

*B*uilding a relationship with my readers is one the things I enjoy best. I occasionally send out messages about new releases, special offers, discount codes and other bits of news relating to my various series.

And for a limited time, I'll send you copy of BUNDLE OF TROU-BLE: Book 1 in the MATERNAL INSTINCTS MYSTERY SERIES.

Join now

ABOUT THE AUTHOR

*D*iana Orgain is the bestselling author of the *Maternal Instincts Mystery Series,* the *Love or Money Mystery Series,* and the *Roundup Crew Mysteries.* She is the co-author of NY Times Best-selling *Scrapbooking Mystery Series* with Laura Childs. For a complete listing of books, as well as excerpts and contests, and to connect with Diana:

Visit Diana's website at www.dianaorgain.com.

Join Diana reader club and newsletter and get Free books here

CPSIA information can be obtained
at www.ICGtesting.com
Printed in the USA
LVHW051552290122
709584LV00012B/1352